P9-BYS-521

CHANGES

The more Caitlin thought about it, the more she was convinced that the rumor Morgan had told her really was true. She stared hard at the phone and jumped when it suddenly rang. It was Jed.

"I know you must be thinking terrible things about me," Jed said. "Melanie said she told you I was out all night. Honestly, I just slept over at this guy's apartment."

"Oh, so now Nonnie Coe is a *guy!*"

"What!"

"Everyone's talking about you two," Caitlin said bitterly.

"You've got to be joking," Jed sputtered. "I was at Bill's house last night. Call him if you don't believe me."

"I'm sorry, Jed," Caitlin said.

"Can't we at least get together and talk?" Jed persisted.

Caitlin sighed. "Don't bother, Jed."

She replaced the receiver in the cradle. She couldn't forgive Jed for changing so much. He wasn't the same person she had fallen in love with. Somehow he had turned into a person she didn't think she could love anymore. . . .

Bantam Starfire Books in the Caitlin series
Ask your bookseller for the books you have missed

THE LOVE TRILOGY
  Loving
  Love Lost
  True Love

THE PROMISE TRILOGY
  Tender Promises
  Promises Broken
  A New Promise

THE FOREVER TRILOGY
  Dreams of Forever
  Forever and Always (coming in January 1988)
  Together Forever (coming in February 1988)

Caitlin

DREAMS
OF
FOREVER

Created by
Francine Pascal

Written by
Diana Gregory

BANTAM BOOKS
TORONTO · NEW YORK · LONDON · SYDNEY · AUCKLAND

RL 6, IL age 12 and up

DREAMS OF FOREVER
A Bantam Book / December 1987

Conceived by Francine Pascal

Produced by Cloverdale Press, Inc.,
133 Fifth Avenue, New York, NY 10003

The Starfire logo is a registered trademark of Bantam Books, Inc.
Registered in U.S. Patent and Trademark Office and elsewhere.

All rights reserved.
Copyright © 1987 by Francine Pascal.
Cover art copyright © 1987 by Bantam Books, Inc.
This book may not be reproduced in whole or in part, by
mimeograph or any other means, without permission.
For information address: Bantam Books, Inc.

ISBN 0-553-26700-0

Published simultaneously in the United States and Canada

Bantam Books are published by Bantam Books, Inc. Its trademark,
consisting of the words "Bantam Books" and the portrayal of a rooster, is
Registered in U.S. Patent and Trademark Office and in other countries.
Marca Registrada. Bantam Books, Inc., 666 Fifth Avenue, New York,
New York 10103.

PRINTED IN THE UNITED STATES OF AMERICA

O   0 9 8 7 6 5 4 3 2 1

DREAMS
OF
FOREVER

1

"We did it, Caitlin!" Jed Michaels whooped joyfully to the beautiful girl standing in front of him. Then, the excitement still bubbling inside of him, he encircled her waist with his hands and swung her around with such force that the mortarboard flew off her head. Caitlin Ryan's shining dark hair fanned out above her shoulders, while her white graduation gown billowed out from her slender body.

"And I love you," Jed added in a lower, more tender tone as he set her down gently. He pulled her into his arms and looked thoughtfully down at the girl who had been the love of his life since high school. "Just think, Caitlin," he said, his green eyes dancing, "we are now official alumni of Carleton Hill University. I feel ready to take on the world, ready for my life—our lives—to really begin."

"I know, I know." With a happy smile, Caitlin looked up at Jed. "And I want to spend every single minute of mine with you."

"Every single minute?" Jed asked, teasing her and kissing the tip of her nose. "What about all those hours I'll be spending in the law library during the next few years. Columbia isn't going to be easy, you know. And, " he added with a playful grin, "I'll need to be a very good lawyer if I'm going to be able to support you in the lavish style you're used to." He paused for a moment, studying Caitlin's reaction. "Okay, maybe not that lavishly, but I still intend to be the best attorney I can be."

"You'll be wonderful," Caitlin assured him lovingly. Then the expression in her eyes turned serious, the blue darkening to violet. "And you know perfectly well that I couldn't care less about material things—now. Love is far more important than money." She gave a slight shake of her head. "I should know."

"You're never, ever going to lose my love, either," Jed assured her. "That I promise." Then the ebullient mood of graduation day overtook him again. "And what about you, Miss Caitlin Ryan? Or should I call you Brenda Starr, girl reporter?"

"Honestly, Jed!" she remarked, giving him a

playful punch on the arm. "How many times have I told you that I'm only going to be an assistant to one of the editors? My job at *National News* will probably consist of stuff like retyping copy and making coffee. I'm hardly going to be a glamorous reporter. In fact, I just found out that my new boss isn't even in the news department—she's a feature editor."

"But *National* is a news magazine," Jed insisted, his eyes twinkling.

"Yes, but—" Caitlin broke off and began laughing. "Oh, all right. Maybe someday I *will* see something I've written in print. And it might even be a major news story. But that's a long way off."

"Knowing you, that time isn't as far away as you think. In fact, I'll bet you a dollar that within one year you'll have your name in print." Jed smiled. He had complete confidence in Caitlin's ability to reach any goal she set for herself.

"Only a dollar," Caitlin asked. "Why, Jed Michaels, is that all you're willing to wager on me? Why—"

"There you are," a warm, masculine voice said, breaking in on their conversation. Jed and Caitlin stepped apart and turned to greet Dr. Gordon Westlake. Tall and handsome, with clear blue eyes, most people could tell by looking at him that Dr. Westlake was Caitlin's father. The love he felt for her was obvious as well, and he stood beaming at his daughter. Caitlin smiled back at him.

Caitlin hadn't even known her father as long as she had known Jed. Jed and she had met when they were both juniors at Highgate Academy, one of the most prestigious prep schools in Virginia. Caitlin, whose mother had died in childbirth, was raised by her grandmother, Regina Ryan, the wealthy and powerful owner of Ryan Mining. Laura Ryan, Caitlin's mother, had fallen in love with Gordon Westlake, a poor, young medical student. But Mrs. Ryan thought he wouldn't be an appropriate husband for her daughter, so she spirited Laura off to Europe to forget him, only to discover that her daughter was already pregnant with Gordon's child. After Laura died, the grief-stricken Regina Ryan brought Caitlin back to Virginia to raise her. She swore that Caitlin would never know the truth about her father, and she never told Gordon Westlake that he had a daughter. The truth came out, however, when Caitlin and Dr. Westlake accidently met at a hospital where he was the director. After an uneasy beginning, their love had grown steadily, and Caitlin now shared a very close and warm relationship with her father. And their relationship had forced an uneasy truce between Dr. Westlake and Mrs. Ryan.

In fact, Mrs. Ryan was standing just behind

Dr. Westlake as he gave Caitlin a congratulatory hug. Although the weather was muggy and oppressive, Regina Ryan appeared cool and elegant in her jade green linen dress. Her silver hair had been swept back from her face to emphasize her patrician features and steel blue eyes.

In contrast, Jed's father, Carl Michaels, who had also joined the little group, seemed uncomfortably warm. He stood a short distance from Regina Ryan and Gordon Westlake and appeared just slightly out of place. His light tan suit was traditional and perfectly tailored, but it was his expensive western boots and his deeply tanned face that set him apart from the others. He looked like what he was, an extremely successful rancher from Montana who would rather be riding the open range than standing on the university's beautifully tended, formal lawn.

"We've been looking for you two for the past twenty minutes," Dr. Westlake continued. "But then, it's hard to find anyone in this crowd of white caps and gowns." With a chuckle, he added, "Especially when the people you're looking for aren't trying very hard to find you."

"Sorry, sir," Jed said, looking slightly embarrassed, but quickly recovering with a slow grin.

"Honestly, Father!" Caitlin cried, trying to sound indignant while laughing. "Hello, Grandmother," she said, turning to greet Mrs. Ryan. "And, Mr. Michaels, how nice to see you."

"Congratulations, Caitlin," Mr. Michaels replied, smiling at her. Then he turned toward Jed and his smile broadened. "Congratulations, son!" he boomed.

"Thanks, Dad. And thanks for coming. I know how busy you are right now."

"Nonsense. I wouldn't have missed this for anything. Besides, the ranch will still be there when I get back." He smiled self-consciously. "The work, too, I reckon." He turned back to Jed. "I'm just sorry Melanie couldn't be here, but your sister's still in the middle of exams."

"Of course, I understand," Jed said. "Maybe we can give her a call later to wish her luck."

Mr. Michaels nodded. Just then Mrs. Ryan broke into the conversation. "Caitlin, dear, you did look lovely up on the stage when you received your diploma. And I'm very proud of you for making Phi Beta Kappa." She put a slender, perfectly manicured hand over one of Caitlin's, giving it a gentle squeeze. The gesture was the closest Regina Ryan ever came to showing affection in public.

"Jed has earned honors, too, I'm told," Mr. Michaels remarked, clapping his son on the shoulder. As he moved, he winced suddenly.

"Dad?" Jed asked in a concerned tone. "Dad, is something the matter?" He was convinced his father worked too hard for a man his age, and now Jed began to worry that something was seriously wrong.

"It's nothing. Nothing's the matter," Mr. Michaels assured Jed quickly. "I must've sprained something when I was moving all that hay around yesterday morning." He frowned slightly. "I noticed it at the airport yesterday afternoon and then again this morning when I got up."

"Are you sure you're okay, Dad?" Jed's face still reflected his concern.

"Of course I'm sure," his father replied. Then, to steer the conversation away from his health, he turned to Gordon Westlake and Regina Ryan. "I suppose you know I've always wanted Jed to be a rancher—you know, follow in my footsteps. I even asked him to spend one year at agricultural college hoping he'd change his mind. But now I can see that he's going to be a lot happier in a courtroom than riding an old cow pony like his father."

"That horse of yours is hardly an old cow pony," Caitlin reminded him. "She's one of the most beautiful quarter horses I've ever seen." Caitlin reached out to touch his arm.

"Caitlin!" Mrs. Ryan burst out. "Why aren't you wearing the watch I gave you for graduation? Is something wrong with it?"

"Well—no." Caitlin glanced guiltily down at her wrist. Taking a deep breath, she tried to explain herself as diplomatically as possible. "The watch is gorgeous, Grandmother, but it's a little too formal for today. And, maybe, I'm a little young for a diamond watch?"

"Not at all," her grandmother insisted. "A diamond watch is perfectly suitable for an occasion of such importance. And you may be young, but you are no longer a little girl."

"I know," Caitlin said quietly. "Grandmother, I love the watch, I really do. It's one of the most elegant pieces of jewelry you've ever given me, and I am going to wear it. I'll put it on later when we all go out to dinner. But for now, I think the watch is just too dressy."

"Well, I see you didn't think your gift from your father was too dressy to wear," Mrs. Ryan said haughtily.

"It's a little more casual," Caitlin said as she reached up and touched the monogrammed gold disk that hung from a gold chain around her neck. On the back was engraved, "With love always, Father." It had arrived at her sorority house that morning along with an extremely generous check. The accompanying card said that the money was to be used for "the unexpected expenses of independent living." Caitlin smiled. Her father understood her so well— from finding the perfect present for her to remembering what it was like to start out. As much as she hated to hurt her grandmother's feelings, a diamond watch definitely was not her style.

"If you think so," Mrs. Ryan finally conceded. "Now, I think it's time to—" Catching a glimpse of Jed's father, she stopped in midsentence. "Mr. Michaels? Mr. Michaels, are you ill?"

As she spoke, the rest of the small group turned to look at Jed's father. Mr. Michaels started to reply, but instead only gasped. A look of stunned surprise crossed his face before he slumped forward and started to fall toward the ground.

"Dad!" Jed called out, reaching out to help his father. But Mr. Michaels, grimacing now with pain, could not hold on to his son's outstretched hand. Seconds later he was unconscious on the lawn.

"Dad! Dad, say something!" Jed dropped to his knees and slipped one arm beneath his father's head, lifting it. "Dad, can you hear me?" There was no reaction. Looking up at Gordon Westlake, Jed pleaded, "Do something. Please, do something."

Dr. Westlake quickly knelt beside the fallen man. "Move aside," he told Jed kindly but firmly. "Let me look at him." With a dazed look, Jed stood up. Caitlin's father than checked Mr. Michaels for a pulse, and finding none, he began preparations for CPR. As he did so, he said calmly to Caitlin, "I want you to go to a phone and call an ambulance. Tell them a man has suffered a heart attack." As Caitlin turned to go, he added, more to himself than the Caitlin, "And tell them to hurry!"

2

Caitlin felt as though hundreds of tiny grains of sand had been poured into her tired eyes, and her body ached with exhaustion. But looking at Jed slumped in the corner of the orange vinyl waiting-room couch, she knew he felt a hundred times worse. The last time he had looked over at her, his eyes had been dull and filled with the pain of someone caught in the middle of a tragedy.

She wanted so much to go over to him, to sit beside him and comfort him. But Jed had withdrawn into himself, he had put a wall up around himself. Caitlin knew she had to respect his need to be left alone. Nevertheless, she had decided to stay with him in the waiting room, close enough so that if he needed her, she would be there for him.

A paper cup sat on the end table beside her. It was half full of cold coffee. How long had it been since she had gone down to the machines to get that? She wondered. An hour? Two? Was it before midnight? After? The longer she was in that windowless, impersonal room, with its hard, ugly furniture and bright, fluorescent lights, the more blurred the passage of time became.

Caitlin looked at the wall clock over the nurses' station in intensive care. Seven minutes after three. Except for a brief trip to the coffee shop to call Melanie and for a dinner that neither she nor Jed had touched, they had been waiting there for more than eleven hours. And the waiting was far from over. The specialist her father had contacted had told them that all they could do for the moment was to be patient and hope for the best.

Caitlin remembered how pale Jed had become as he'd first listened to Dr. Sharp.

"Your father's condition is being monitored continuously," the tanned, middle-aged man had told Jed. "He still hasn't regained consciousness, but at least that means he's not in any pain, either." The lines on the doctor's forehead deepened. "Your father's condition is quite serious. I won't lie to you about that. I called his physician in Montana, and he confirmed what I had already suspected. He has had a heart condition. Now all that's left for us to do is wait." Numbly, Jed nodded. "The next fifteen to twenty hours are going to be critical. I wish I could offer you more hope than that, but unfortunately I can't." He ran a hand through his graying hair in an absent gesture. "Still, I'm always amazed at the amount of punishment the human body can take and still survive." The doctor managed a weary half smile. "I'll let you know if there's any change."

Caitlin stood up and walked around, replaying the first frantic minutes of the tragedy in her mind. An ambulance had arrived almost immediately, and the ride to the hospital was quick. But after that, it seemed as though everything moved in slow motion. Mr. Michaels was in the examining room in the emergency room for an exceptionally long time, during which no one knew whether he would even survive long enough for the doctors to run their tests. Restlessly, the four of them had paced the waiting area.

Finally, when Mr. Michaels had been taken to the intensive care ward, Jed had been allowed to go in and see him for a few moments. When he was gone, Mrs. Ryan pulled Caitlin aside to urge her to go back to the hotel.

"You need to get some rest, dear," she insisted. "Jed or the doctor will call if there's any news." But Caitlin had steadfastly refused to go.

She wanted to stay with Jed. Her father, however, understood how Caitlin felt, and he finally persuaded Regina to go back to the Gaylord Hotel, where they had all taken rooms for the night. He would accompany her.

After they had left, Caitlin waited alone until Jed rejoined her. Seeing the stricken look on his face, she had rushed over to him and led him back to the couch.

"Oh, Caitlin . . ." Jed's voice had been strained. He spoke in a voice that was so low she could barely hear him. "My dad looks so terrible. He's so pale." Jed had shook his head, his eyes glistening with tears. "He looks so—so helpless."

"Jed. Jed," Caitlin had crooned softly, drawing him into her arms. "I'm so sorry." She didn't know what else to say. She couldn't bring herself to tell Jed that his father would be all right; Caitlin honestly feared that Mr. Michaels might not recover.

"Oh, Caitlin, I never should have asked him to make the trip here for graduation. I should have known it would be too much for him." Jed had shuddered miserably. "God, he'd still be fine if he'd stayed at home on the ranch."

"Don't torture yourself this way." She had taken his hand, forcing him to look at her. "Listen to me. Your father could have had that heart attack anywhere—back at the ranch, any-

14

where. And my father made sure that he has the best cardiologist on the East Coast taking care of him." She tightened her hold on his hand. "Besides, Jed, you know your father wanted to come. He's proud of you."

Jed nodded. "I thought I was a terrible disappointment to him because I won't be a rancher. After all, he built the ranch for his family. And now, if he—if he dies—there'll be no one left to run it."

"Stop it, Jed!" Caitlin's voice had been firm, but her eyes were filled with concern. She reached up and gently touched Jed's cheek. "Ranching isn't right for you. Your father finally understands that."

"Still, maybe I should have tried harder. Maybe—"

"You did everything you could, Jed. You spent a year at Montana Agricultural College just to please him."

"I know, but—I don't know, Caitlin." Jed had stared blankly across the room at the opposite wall. "He's lying in there, maybe dying, and I feel so guilty. I've been so incredibly self-centered recently, ignoring my father's wishes and caring only about what I wanted to do with my life."

"That's normal, Jed," Caitlin had insisted tenderly. "You have to live your own life. Everyone does. If you had tried to be what your father

15

wanted you to be, you'd have been miserable. And then your father'd have been the one who felt guilty."

Jed had turned to face Caitlin, his eyes narrowing thoughtfully. "I'm not so positive that I would have been miserable. Now that I think about it, I think I could be happy on the ranch. I loved it there, I still do."

"Of course you do, but you're confusing the future with the past." She had looked deep into his eyes. "I know you, Jed Michaels. These past three years at college, you've lived and breathed the law. You've seemed obsessed by it sometimes. No, Jed, don't punish yourself by thinking about what might have been." She had given him a quick, nervous smile to lighten the moment.

Then like a door shutting her out, the faraway look came back into Jed's eyes. "I don't want to talk anymore, Caitlin," he said softly.

That had been hours before. Perhaps she should forget her promise to herself to leave Jed alone, Caitlin thought. If only she could break through his silent brooding. It was so hard, watching him, seeing the way he was hurting. She was just about to go over to him when her eye was caught by swift, hurried movement out in the corridor. Jed saw it, too. He was on his feet in seconds.

Several people ran into Mr. Michaels's room,

while at the same time the calm, impersonal voice of the hospital's central operator came over the intercom. "Dr. Sharp to ICU. Dr. Sharp to ICU. Stat. Code blue. Code blue. Dr. Sharp. . ."

"No, please, no," Jed whispered hoarsely. Caitlin had rushed to his side, and together they stood watching as a team of men and women in hospital uniforms wheeled a cart filled with equipment into Mr. Michaels's room. Caitlin overheard someone call it a "crash cart," and because her father was a doctor, she knew what it meant. The machine being wheeled into Jed's father's room was used to get a person's heart beating again once it had stopped.

Caitlin's own heart was pounding as she continued to watch the door to Jed's father's room. The operator was still calling Dr. Sharp's name over the loudspeaker. Finally he came running down the corridor past Caitlin and Jed. He went straight into Mr. Michael's room, with not so much as a glance at either of them.

"Caitlin," Jed said slowly. She looked up at him and saw he was deathly pale. "Caitlin, I-I'm so scared!"

"I'm sorry," Dr. Sharp offered in a quiet tone some time later. Caitlin was standing beside Jed, her hand touching his arm, reassuring him that she was there. "We did everything we could."

"I'm sure you did," Jed replied, nodding numbly. "And thank you for coming all the way from Washington. I—I appreciate it."

Dr. Sharp glanced over at Caitlin. "I really must be going, but please give my best to your father. He left the hospital before I could speak with him." The doctor then turned and walked back down the hall.

"Come on, Jed. Let's go," Caitlin urged gently a few minutes after Dr. Sharp had left. Jed did not move. He continued to stand in the same spot, as if he weren't sure of what to do next. "Let's go back to the hotel and get some sleep. There's nothing to do here that can't wait until the morning." She slid her hand up to rest on his shoulder. "You should get a couple of hours of sleep. We could both use some."

"You're right. But I don't feel like going back to the hotel. Not yet. I just want to get out of here. Maybe I'll go for a walk." He looked at her, noticing for the first time how tired she must be. The fine skin beneath her eyes was dark from exhaustion. "You go ahead, though. Here, I'll call a cab for you." He started toward the phone booth.

"No, Jed," Caitlin replied, reaching out to stop him. "I want to stay with you. Unless," she added in a hesitant tone, "you'd rather be alone."

"No, to be honest, I don't want to be alone," Jed admitted. "But I do want to walk and think."

"Then I'll walk with you."

As they left the hospital, Caitlin noticed the sky was already turning from navy to blue gray. The air was cool, though, and dew dampened the stretch of lawn between the hospital building and the sidewalk. Walking toward the street, she took several deep breaths. The clean, fresh morning air was a welcome change after the stuffiness of the hospital.

At the end of the hospital driveway, they turned onto the sidewalk and continued on for several minutes. Finally Jed spoke. "It's so hard to believe, Caitlin. At this time the day before yesterday my dad was at the ranch, getting ready to come here, probably giving some last-minute instructions to the foreman. He was alive, doing things, and now he's dead. There's such a fine line." Jed shrugged helplessly. "Now who's going to give the instructions at the ranch? Who'll make the decisions?"

Caitlin didn't answer right away. Then, after a long moment, she asked, "What about Melanie?"

"Melanie?" Jed sounded surprised. Then he shook his head. "No, she's no good at ranching," he said, misinterpreting Caitlin's question.

"No, Jed," Caitlin said gently. "I meant when

do you plan on calling her? You have to tell her about your father."

"Oh, yes, that. Of course. I'll call her later. There's no reason to wake her up with the bad news."

"But don't you think she's been awake all night, just as we have? She's probably been going crazy worrying ever since you called."

"I didn't tell her how serious it was," Jed admitted. "I didn't want to upset her when there wasn't anything she could do, I just told her that he wasn't feeling well and he'd been taken to the hospital for tests. I said I'd call her back this morning." He sighed. "I hate having to tell her this over the phone."

"Isn't there someone you could call?" Caitlin asked. "Someone who could come and stay with Melanie until you get back. Maybe Eve," she suggested. Eve was Melanie's best friend, as well as Jed's ex-girlfriend.

"That's a good idea. Thanks." Jed looked dispirited. "I should have thought about that."

"When do you think you'll leave?" Caitlin asked, putting her hand on his arm.

"I guess I'll go back this afternoon," he said as he looked around at the day that was taking shape. "In a few hours."

They came to a bridge that formed a highway overpass. Jed paused, turning to stare at the headlights of the early-morning traffic that streamed below them. Stopping to stand beside him, Caitlin watched his expression. As she looked, a terrible sense of unease washed over her. Jed was trying to come to some kind of decision, she was sure of that. Finally he turned to her.

"Caitlin—" he said, reaching for her hand. "What would you say if I told you I might decide to stay on in Montana to take care of the ranch?"

Jed's words didn't completely surprise Caitlin, and yet she wasn't quite prepared for them, either. Fragments of thought went flying through her head: *My job at the magazine . . . Jed's classes at Columbia . . . the excitement of living in New York City . . . the friends we'd meet . . .* She looked over at Jed, studying him. The sun was coming up then, bringing out streaks of gold in his light brown hair and softening the green of his eyes. Right then, Caitlin knew she had her answer. Quietly she said, "You asked me what I would say?"

"Yes," Jed said, his voice low and unsure.

"I'd say I'm coming with you."

"Oh, Caitlin, I love you," Jed whispered with relief. He slid his arms around her, pulling her to him. They just held each other for a long, long time.

3

Jed's father was buried four days later in a small cemetery not far from the ranch where he had spent most of his life. Over the years Mr. Michaels had made many friends, and the guests at his funeral included not only the president of the Cattleman's Association, but the lieutenant governor of the state of Montana as well.

The arrangements that had to be made for the funeral helped to take Jed's mind off his grief. At the same time he was continuing to wrestle with the idea of returning to Montana permanently. He had thought the decision would be easy once he was back home, surrounded by familiar people and sights. But they only served to confuse him more. He was drawn to the places of his childhood—he found comfort in them. At the same time, he knew he would miss the life he and Caitlin were about to begin in New York.

During all this time Caitlin stood silently beside Jed, telling herself that she had to allow him the freedom to work things out on his own. It was obvious to her that the only reason Jed was considering staying in Montana was that he felt guilty because he hadn't gone into ranching. And now that his father was dead, Jed was trying to ease his guilt by doing exactly what he had successfully fought against for so long. Caitlin was sure that Jed, too, would realize this before long.

On the day after the funeral, however, the decision to stay or go was taken out of Jed's hands.

The family attorney, a man named Anthony Stone, had asked Jed and Melanie to meet with him in his office to go over Mr. Michaels's will. Caitlin had not gone because Jed had told her the meeting would be short, just a formality. Jed had kissed her and left, promising to be back soon.

Caitlin spent the morning curled up on one of the long leather couches in the living room of the rambling ranch house, a house that Jed's father had designed to nestle into the base of the mountains that formed the western boundary of the thirteen-thousand acre cattle spread. Except for Mrs. Mallory, the housekeeper, who was working in the kitchen at the far end of the house, Caitlin was alone. The house was so quiet that the sound of the pages turning as she flipped through a copy of *Quarter Horse Journal* seemed to echo in the huge room. Something was wrong, Caitlin could feel it. They had been gone far too long. Finally she heard the sound of the pickup pull up to the house and the engine shut off.

Jumping up, she ran to meet Jed. The furious expression on his face as he stepped through the front door, however, made her stop in the hall, some five feet from him. "Jed!" she gasped. "Jed, what is it? What's happened?" Caitlin turned toward Melanie, who had come in right behind him. She looked almost as stricken. Without a glance toward Caitlin, she brushed past both of them and hurried down the hall in the direction of her room. Seconds later Caitlin heard the slam of Melanie's bedroom door. "Jed?" she repeated, taking a step closer. "What's going on?"

"It's gone. All of it—gone." Jed's voice when he finally spoke was an agonizing rasp. "The ranch is gone."

"Wh-what?" Caitlin cried. She stared at him, incredulous. "I don't believe it. There has to be a mistake."

"No, there's no mistake." Jed's tone had turned bitter. He closed his eyes as if to shut out

24

the memory of what had occurred at the lawyer's office. Then he opened them again and walked past Caitlin and went into the living room. She followed him, sitting down on the leather couch again as he slumped in a chair across from her. Jed took a deep breath, then let the air out of his lungs in a long sigh. He looked over at Caitlin. "My dad left the ranch to my mother. It's hers now."

Suddenly she fully understood Jed's bitterness. Caitlin remembered when she had first started dating Jed and he told her about his mother. He had explained that when he was a freshman in high school, she had deserted them all, running off to California to live with a Hollywood producer. And in the years since then, she had never once made a phone call to her husband or children. Caitlin shook her head, wondering how Jed's father could possibly have left the ranch to such a horrible woman.

"Oh, Jed," Caitlin finally said. "I'm sorry. So very, very sorry." Rising, she went over and knelt beside his chair, putting her hand on his knee. "But how could he have done such a thing?"

"I don't think he meant to," Jed replied, shaking his head. "Not after what she did." Jed's eyes flashed with anger. "Mr. Stone told me that he'd been trying to get my father to update his will for years. But he just kept putting it off.

Maybe he thought he was immortal. Or maybe he just didn't want to think about dying." Distractedly, Jed ran his hand through his hair. "God, you'd think he would have done something about it after he found out he had a heart condition!"

"Did he leave everything to your mother?" Caitlin asked in a soft voice.

"No, only the ranch." Jed shrugged wearily. "The rest—some stocks, bonds, and about eight hundred acres of land in New Mexico—are to be divided equally between Melanie and me. According to Mr. Stone, we'll have a large enough income from those investments that neither of us will have to worry for years."

Caitlin was silent for a moment, considering what Jed had said. One question burned in her mind, and she finally summoned the courage to ask it. "Do you think your mother will want to move back here? You know, and run the ranch?"

"Are you joking!" Jed let out a short laugh. "The last thing my mother would want to do is come back here. No, the ranch is as good as sold actually. Apparently Mr. Stone told my mother about the will a couple of days ago and she contacted some people who've been wanting to buy it for a long time. Mr. Stone didn't want to bother Melanie and me with the details until after the funeral because he thought it would just upset us even more." Jed sighed. "Nice guy, huh."

"Jed, you said the ranch was *as good as* sold," Caitlin said, looking up at him. "Does that mean there's a chance that it isn't yet?"

"No. It's just that it takes time to draw up the papers and transfer the property. But the ranch is definitely gone or will be soon."

"She didn't just sell it, either!" Melanie, her voice harsh and strident, stood in the doorway. Caitlin swung around to look across the room at Jed's younger sister—a slender, feminine version of Jed. "She sold the ranch to a lousy group of investors. Now there won't be anyone here to love this place—not like Dad did. Oh, I hate her! I hate her so—so much!" Melanie's voice wavered, and she began crying. She buried her face in her hands while violent sobs shook her slender shoulders.

Standing up quickly, Caitlin crossed the room and put her arms around Melanie, allowing Melanie to bury her head against her shoulder. Gently rubbing Melanie's back, Caitlin wished Jed could let go of his anger and guilt the same way. He had been so calm and in control that it almost frightened Caitlin. And Caitlin knew that his grief had to come out eventually—one way or another.

Caitlin's fears continued into that evening as she and Jed took a walk together. She talked only about practical matters with him, matters dealing with the sale of the ranch.

"They asked Mr. Stone if I'd stay here for a while," he told her. "To make the changeover as smooth as possible. I've decided I'm going to. My dad would have wanted me to."

They were down near the barn. The sun had gone down about half an hour earlier, and the twilight had turned everything around them a soft shade of lavender gray. The field crickets were beginning to chirp and a bullfrog down at the pond added his voice occasionally. Caitlin paused to lean against one of the rails of the corral. Dressed in jeans and a loose white shirt, she had her hair pinned to the top of her head. A few loose tendrils were blowing softly across her face in the light evening breeze.

"How long do you think you'll have to stay?" she asked.

"Not too long," Jed replied after thinking for a moment. "I'd guess about three or four weeks, maybe a bit longer. I promise I'll come straight to New York as soon as I can." He brushed the wisps of hair away from her face and gently cupped her head in his hand. "I'm going to miss you horribly. Are you sure you won't stay here with me? Then we could fly to New York together."

"You know I'd love that, Jed," she said in a warm voice. "But now that we're going ahead with our original plans, I have a job waiting for me. I'm supposed to report to work first thing

Monday morning, and it's already Thursday."
She put both her arms around his waist and slid
her hands into the back pockets of his jeans. "I
should leave no later than tomorrow morning.
Even then I'll barely have time to go to Ryan
Acres and sort out what I want to have shipped
and what I want to take with me."

"I know," Jed conceded. "Still I thought I'd
ask. No harm in that, is there?"

"Only because it makes me wish I could say
yes," Caitlin replied.

"Melanie's going to be sorry to see you go,
too. You've been so understanding with her—
more understanding than I seem capable of
being right now."

"She knows how hard you're trying, Jed."
Caitlin smiled tenderly at him. "Besides, I think
Melanie needs another woman to talk to right
now." Caitlin frowned slightly before adding,
"You know, I'm really concerned about her.
What's going to happen to her when you move
to New York? Oh, I know she has friends here,
and she's going back to Montana State in the fall,
but friends aren't the same as family. I mean,
what will she do on long weekends? And what
about Thanksgiving and Christmas? Jed, she's
going to need a place to call home."

"Yeah, I know. I've been thinking about that,
too," Jed admitted. "But I don't know what I can
do from New York."

"Well, what if she transferred to a school like New York University? It's in the city, and that way she could live with you," Caitlin suggested. It seemed like the perfect solution. "She's interested in being a communications major, right?" Jed nodded. "Well, New York is the best place in the world for someone who's interested in that kind of thing."

"You have this all figured out, don't you?" Jed looked at the satisfied grin on Caitlin's face and couldn't help adding lightly, "And what decisions have you made for me?"

It was the first time since that horrible day almost a week before that Jed had teased her. Caitlin's heart lifted. But then Jed's expression turned serious again. "There's only one problem. I'm not sure she'll want to transfer. I mean, she's lived in Montana all her life. New York would be a pretty scary place for someone like her."

"I'll talk to her if you want," Caitlin offered. "We really communicate well."

"That would be great, Caitlin. Did you know that I think you're wonderful?" Jed's soft smile was genuine. He slid his arms around her and pressed her to him. Breathing warmly against her neck, he whispered, "What would I ever do without you?"

"I hope you'll never have to find out," she replied, her voice low and warm as his. "Oh,

Jed—" She ran her hands along the strong, corded muscles of his back, hugging him to her. "Please, please don't stay here in Montana a second longer than you have to."

"Don't worry." Jed leaned back and looked into Caitlin's deep blue eyes. "I couldn't stay away from you one moment longer than necessary if I tried." Then he leaned down and kissed her, gently and lovingly, sealing his promise.

Caitlin flew home to Ryan Acres the next morning. Before she left, however, she spoke to Melanie. It had taken an hour and a half of talking, but Caitlin had finally managed to convince her to come to New York with Jed at the end of the summer. She'd enroll at NYU if she could get in. If not, she'd stay out a semester. Caitlin had promised Melanie she'd talk to the admissions people about what Melanie had to do. It was a small favor and she was glad to do it. After all, someday Melanie would be her sister-in-law. Sitting in her seat on the plane, the remains of the airline lunch still on the pull-down tray in front of her, Caitlin smiled to herself. Melanie would be her sister-in-law, and Jed would be her husband. Yes, she liked the sound of that.

It was early evening by the time Caitlin arrived at Ryan Acres. Her flight had landed at Dulles Airport in Washington, D.C., at five-fifteen, and Rollins, the family butler and driver, had met her in the Bentley and driven her home. Caitlin was disappointed to find out her grandmother wouldn't be there to greet her. Mrs. Ryan had gone to Richmond on business and would not be back until the following afternoon. Tired, Caitlin had ordered a tray to be sent up to her, then gone to her room. She'd taken a long, soaking bath, put on silk pajamas, and crawled into bed to eat her light supper.

When Caitlin woke up, sunlight was streaming in through the windows. She had forgotten to pull the blue brocade drapes closed the night before. Opening her eyes, she was disappointed to find herself in her bedroom at Ryan Acres. She had been dreaming she was still in Montana with Jed. *But I'm not, am I,* she thought, resolutely sliding her feet into a pair of pale yellow silk slippers and padding across the room to the bathroom.

Of course I'm not, she repeated to herself, turning on the faucet in the shower, pulling off her pajamas, and stepping under the warm needles of water. *But it won't be long before we're together again. Only a few short weeks. What had Jed said, three? Four? Well, I can wait. I've waited for him before.*

Sorting through her clothes and deciding

which items she wanted to take to New York took longer than she had expected. Dressed in shorts and a tank top, her hair pulled haphazardly into a ponytail, she was exhausted by the time she finished. Slumping down onto the carpet, Caitlin leaned against her bed and looked at the boxes of things she had decided to leave stored at Ryan Acres.

Sticking out of one of the boxes was a photo album of her favorite snapshots from both high school and college. Leaning forward, she reached into the box and pulled the album out. She suddenly wanted to find one particular photo. Settling back against the side of the bed again, she flipped through the pages, stopping a couple of times to look at photos of herself and Jed. Some had been taken at Highgate and some at Carleton Hill. Caitlin forced herself to turn the page and not dwell on her memories of Jed. At last she found the photograph she was looking for. The color print was of three girls—herself and two friends from Highgate—Gloria Parks and Morgan Conway.

Caitlin ran a finger lightly over the surface of the photo. It had been taken in the fall of their junior year. Gloria and Morgan were always together, sharing gossip and care packages full of junk food from home. Morgan, especially, she remembered, was crazy about anything with chocolate in it. Caitlin laughed. She had heard recently that Morgan had become a confirmed health nut and lost twenty pounds. What else had changed? Caitlin wondered.

Well, she would find out soon enough. Morgan and Gloria were sharing an apartment in New York, and they had offered to let her stay with them until she found an apartment of her own.

4

Riding through the clogged streets of New York in the back seat of a cab whose upholstery had seen better days, Caitlin looked at the city that would now be her home, a city she had only visited in the past.

"We'll be there soon, miss," the cabbie called over his shoulder. Moments later he honked loudly at a bus that had just cut him off. "Jerk!" he hissed. Then he turned his attention back to Caitlin again. "You're just moving to New York, aren't you? Even without all the suitcases, I can always tell." Before Caitlin could respond the cabbie pressed the horn again, this time raising his hand and shaking it at someone Caitlin couldn't see. "The Upper East Side's a nice neighborhood. That where you going to live?"

"Yes," Caitlin said to avoid being rude. She

turned and looked out the window at all the high-rise buildings and thought about Morgan and Gloria and what they had told her they'd been doing since the three of them were at Highgate together.

Morgan, who had gone to college in Boston, had enrolled in an accelerated program, so that she'd graduated in three years instead of four. After her junior year, Gloria had decided to take some time off in order to decide if she really wanted to get her degree in political science, as she had planned. When Morgan had decided to move to New York, Gloria, who had been living in the city with her aunt, suggested they get a place together. And, as far as Caitlin could tell from their letters and phone conversations, they were having a great time.

Now, as the cab pulled up in front of a beautiful old brick building, Caitlin smiled to herself. In just a few minutes she would be filled in on the latest happenings in their lives.

"Okay, miss," the cabbie said, looking at Caitlin in the rearview mirror. "Here it is. That's twenty-one dollars even."

Twenty minutes later, after Morgan and Gloria had helped her wrestle her suitcases into the elevator and up to the ninth floor, Caitlin was sitting on the living room couch sipping a tall glass of iced tea.

Morgan, whose blonde hair had been cut very short, sat across from her in a comfortable chair, a bold yellow-and-green print that matched the throw pillows on the couch. Gloria sat beside Caitlin, with one leg pulled up and tucked beneath her so that she could sit facing her friend.

"I really love your apartment," Caitlin said, looking at the colorful prints on the walls and the lush blue carpet. "It's absolutely darling. It makes me want to hurry up and find my own place."

"Well, how do you like that?" Morgan looked at Gloria and pretended to be hurt. "She's here two seconds, and already she's thinking about moving out."

"I know. How rude!" Gloria agreed, nodding her head, her wheat-colored fuzzy curls bouncing like individual corkscrews. But then she broke into giggles, sounding just as she had when the three of them had been in school together and gossiping in Caitlin's room before lights out. "Seriously, though," Gloria added, "don't you dare think about finding your own place for a while. If nothing else, it's going to take us at least a month to really catch up on what's been happening with you since Highgate. Letters and an occasional lunch or party just don't do the trick. Right, Morgan?"

"Oh, absolutely." Morgan leaned forward. "I want to hear everything—especially things about that gorgeous boyfriend of yours."

"You mean Jed?" Caitlin asked with an innocent smile.

"Is there someone else?" Morgan asked, smelling a bit of gossip.

"Don't be dense, Morgan," Gloria said. "Of course it's Jed. It's always been Jed." She looked at Caitlin. "And I would bet my next six months salary it always will be." She nodded, sure of herself. "So, how long is it going to be before you two get married?"

"You're right about Jed being the one for me forever," Caitlin replied with a happy laugh. "But don't start shopping for wedding presents just yet. We both agreed not to even discuss marriage until he's finished with law school and started working in a law firm."

"Hmmm, too bad," Morgan commented. "That means you won't be asking me to be one of your bridesmaids for at least another three years. I'm not sure I can wait that long."

"And what makes you think Caitlin's even going to ask you," Gloria countered. "Maybe she's got friends from college she'd rather ask."

Caitlin put up her hands to stop them. "I promise, right now, that you can both be in my wedding, okay?"

"Great!" Morgan cried. Then a thoughtful expression came over her face. "What color scheme do you think you'll want? I look really best in pale yellow—but then, if you want—"

"Morgan, honestly!" Gloria laughed.

"Enough about me. What about you two?" Caitlin asked. "Any interesting prospects?"

"Not for me," Morgan replied. "I'm having too much fun to stick with just one guy. But Gloria's fallen into the boring one-man-for-me rut." She wrinkled her nose disdainfully, then added, "No, really, I've got to admit that Rob Hathaway gives new meaning to the word wonderful. If only I'd seen him first—"

"You'd have passed him right by," Gloria said with an easy smile. "He's cute, but definitely not flashy enough for you."

"So, tell me about him," Caitlin said, turning to Gloria. "I'm dying to hear."

"Well, okay." A look of bliss came over Gloria's face as she started talking about Rob. "As you know, I'm working in a law firm as a legal secretary to see if I really like the law and politics—" Caitlin nodded. Gloria had told her about her job during a phone conversation several months earlier. "Well, Rob is a junior partner in the law firm where I work. He's incredibly smart, too. He graduated from Columbia Law only a few years ago. Normally it takes years to be promoted to junior partner."

"Wow, I'm impressed!" Caitlin said. "What does he look like?"

"Well, he's not Mr. Gorgeous or anything," Gloria said. "He's short and has dark hair, and he's kind of reserved, most of the time. But you should see him in court. There he's dynamite." She smiled softly. "But the best thing about Rob is that he encourages me. He really listens to me, to what I think." She shook her head. "You've got to admit that there aren't very many guys out there like that." Caitlin smiled in agreement. That was one of the things she loved about Jed, too. "He convinced me to start taking night classes so I can earn my poli-sci degree. Then I hope to go on to Columbia and study law."

"That's fabulous!" Caitlin exclaimed. "You know, Jed's starting at Columbia this fall. You guys can trade horror stories about law school."

"Great," Gloria agreed. Then she rolled her eyes. "But it's going to be a long time before I'm even finished with my undergrad degree."

Morgan spoke up. "I keep telling her it's worth it, though." She shrugged. "But, of course, there's always the possibility that she'll just get married. The way I'd do it if I were Gloria," Morgan told Caitlin, "would be to marry Rob and then campaign for him when he starts his political career. And after he was elected to Congress, we'd move into an adorable little house in Georgetown."

"Why stop there," Caitlin joked. "Why not run for president?"

"Hey," Morgan said with a toss of her head, "if he had me behind him, who knows. But then, I'm not sure I'd want that kind of life—you know, doing everything behind the scenes for someone else. And I definitely wouldn't give up my own career for anything or anyone." She looked smug. "Just wait, one of these days you're both going to tell everyone you knew me when."

"When what?" Gloria cracked in a friendly, joking way. "When you were secretary at *City Scene*, and you put the outgoing mail into the shredder instead of through the stamp machine?" She looked at Caitlin. "She did that— she really did. Good thing it didn't turn out to be anything too important—just a flyer on new advertising rates."

"So, all right," Morgan said, shrugging. "That should have told management right away that I didn't belong in a clerical position. I didn't go to college to type someone's letters and answer the phone," she explained. "When I first came to New York, I checked out every magazine, and I decided *City Scene* was where I wanted to work. But it's small, and the only opening they had was for a secretary. So that's what I applied for."

"And of course, personnel took one look at

her in her Liz Claiborne dress and knew she would make a perfect secretary."

Caitlin laughed. "So what happened after the stamp-machine incident?"

"Well, I had a choice: either throw myself under a truck, or go to work as a secretary for some other magazine." Morgan paused, and Caitlin laughed. "Actually I came home and went back to my old behavior. I ate an entire Sara Lee cheesecake. Then I started thinking, and I ended up writing a funny piece on what I'd done. And I submitted it to the editor. What the heck, right? I was either going to be fired, or they'd move me out of that stupid clerical job."

"And they promoted you?" Caitlin asked eagerly.

"Um-hmm," Morgan said, nodding. "One assignment just led to another until finally the woman who was writing "Tattle on the Town" accepted a job in London, and I got the column. It is, if I may say so, just about the best gossip column in town."

"I hate to admit it," Gloria said. "But it is a good column." Then she offset her praise somewhat by adding, "Of course, Morgan's been practicing to be a gossip columnist for years."

They all laughed.

"Well, okay," Morgan agreed, smiling broadly. "And I'm still the best." She looked over at Caitlin. "And if you ever want to know anything about who's doing what around town, all you have to do is come ask me."

"I'll remember that," Caitlin promised.

"Hey, you two," Gloria said suddenly, looking at her watch, "it's almost eight o'clock. And I still have a pile of homework to do for my class tomorrow night." She glanced toward the stack of Caitlin's luggage near the front door. "And you've got to unpack. I can't promise that we'll be able to find room for all your clothes, though."

"Yeah," Morgan chimed in, "closet space in New York apartments isn't as plentiful as it is at Ryan Acres. But we can push a little here, shove a little there. Who knows? Miracles have happened."

Gloria stood up. "I'll tell you what: you guys try to perform closet miracles, and I'll attempt to perform a miracle and make dinner." She stretched. "It's been so hot today, how does a nice cool chicken salad and maybe some muffins sound?"

"That sounds heavenly," Caitlin replied.

"Good," Gloria said, heading for the kitchen. Looking back over her shoulder, she added, "Now if I can only remember how my mother makes chicken salad."

5

Caitlin's first week in New York flew by in a blur. She had intended to look for her own apartment—in spite of Morgan's promises that her network of friends would turn one up for her. And even though she did circle the ads in the paper each morning, she hadn't made one call. Her new job took up just about all her energy.

Working at *National News* was exciting at times and dull at others. But it was always frantic because of the rush of activities that went into putting out a weekly news magazine. "Deadline" was the word of the day, every day.

Her office, if it could be called an office, turned out to be a space about five feet by six feet that was only partially walled off from a busy hallway. The space was just large enough to hold Caitlin's gray metal desk and chair, plus a small bookcase, already stacked high with outdated memos and file folders filled with research material that should have been sorted through. Between typing chores, Caitlin organized everything. She also brought in some plants and put her favorite silver-framed photo of Jed at the corner of her desk.

The dull part of her job was the endless typing and retyping of the copy that Arlene Healey, her boss, dropped with constant regularity into her In box. Usually the pages had little yellow notes attached to them that said "Rush." Caitlin would just be starting to type some copy when Arlene would poke her head around the side of the partition and ask in breathless tones, "Have you finished that typing I left for you?"

Caitlin's job also consisted of spending hours on the phone trying to track down some small bit of information or verify a statement before a piece could go into print. She joked to Gloria on Thursday evening, as they were fixing hamburgers for dinner, that boxers weren't the only ones who got cauliflower ears as a result of their jobs. "See!" She pulled back her hair to uncover one ear. "Doesn't this ear look different?"

"Nope," Gloria replied, barely giving Caitlin's ear a glance before she opened the refrigerator and took out some salad fixings. "Looks the same as it always has."

"And then I've got this sore muscle in my

neck from holding the phone to my shoulder when I'm taking messages."

"Awww." Gloria stood up and handed Caitlin a head of lettuce. "Here, see if you can muster up the energy to tear this up and put it in that salad bowl over there."

Caitlin took the lettuce and went to the sink to wash it first. "Are you trying to tell me that you don't have even one tiny bit of sympathy for me?" she asked over her shoulder, a smile touching the corners of her mouth.

"Well, maybe a tiny bit," Gloria answered, grinning back. "Face it, Caitlin, the days of hot and cold running service are over." She returned to the stove to flip the hamburgers. "Gourmet cooking, too, I'm afraid. Uh—I hope you like your burger well done."

"I wouldn't have it any other way," Caitlin said. Then, still holding the lettuce, she went over to the stove to look over Gloria's shoulder. "Working I mean. And I certainly don't mind not having servants. A cook wouldn't hurt, though." She wrinkled her nose. "Well, maybe catsup will help."

By late Friday afternoon Caitlin was ready to go home and take a long soak in the tub before spending the evening curled up with a good book.

Gloria and Morgan, however, were going out for the evening. Gloria had a date with Rob to see an off-Broadway play, while Morgan was going to the opening of a one-man art show at one of the smaller galleries on Madison Avenue. She had met the artist before and was hoping to get a chance to speak with him again. After that, she told Caitlin, she was meeting a couple of friends for dinner. "Why don't you come along? I'm sure my friends would love to meet you."

"Thanks," Caitlin said. "I appreciate the offer, but next time, okay?" She stifled a yawn. "I'm exhausted."

Morgan smiled sympathetically. "I almost forgot, you're not used to the nine-to-five routine. Don't worry, before long you'll be able to work all day and then dance until dawn." Grabbing her purse, she headed for the door, adding, "Promise you'll come next time?"

"I promise," Caitlin replied with a light laugh.

"Good!" Morgan flashed a conspiratorial wink at Caitlin and then flew out the door.

Jed called just after six-thirty. Caitlin was in the kitchen, pouring a can of Diet Coke in a glass. She picked up the receiver, and hearing Jed's familiar voice, she carried the whole phone into the living room. Curling up on the couch, she settled down for a nice, long talk.

But Jed's usual, comfortable drawl was hurried as he said hello to her. It was as if he wanted to get the call over with quickly.

"Is something wrong?" Caitlin asked finally. Her heart jumped fearfully in her chest.

"There sure is!" he said seriously. Then, just as Caitlin's mind was starting to race through a list of possible tragedies, Jed spoke again. "What's wrong is that I miss you terribly."

Relieved, Caitlin let out a deep breath, which she had been holding in. "W-well I miss you, too," she said at last. "But, Jed, do you realize you just frightened me half to death?"

"I did? I'm sorry," Jed apologized. Then he continued quickly. "Look, I can't talk for very long. I just called to see if you have any special plans for this weekend?"

"This weekend?" Caitlin asked in confusion. "Uh—no. Why?"

"Well, if you want some company," Jed offered, "I can be there in time for late breakfast tomorrow morning."

"Really? Oh, Jed, that would be wonderful." A surge of happiness ran through her. "But—but how? What about the ranch? Is everything taken care of?"

"I wish I could say it was," Jed replied, sighing. "No, I've just begun to get things in order." He paused. "And I'm afraid it's going to take longer than I thought at first. But I couldn't bear the thought of being separated from you for that long. So, I made some calls and found out that there are some connecting flights that can get me into New York tomorrow morning." He was silent for a moment. "Well, what do you think?"

"Oh, Jed, I can't wait to see you," Caitlin cried.

"Me, either," Jed assured her in a warm voice. "I knew you'd feel the same way, so I'm at the airport right now. My flight's just been called. I'll stay over in Cleveland tonight and fly out first thing in the morning. There wasn't a way I could get into New York tonight. Love you," he added just before hanging up.

For a long moment Caitlin continued to hold on to the phone. Then she put it back in the cradle and leaned back, looking up at the ceiling. Where, she wondered, should she take Jed for breakfast?

"You couldn't have picked a nicer place," Jed said as he popped the last bite of his croissant into his mouth. Then he wiped the buttery, flaky crumbs off his hand.

"Well, I thought it was appropriate considering the fact that you've just flown in from Montana," Caitlin said. She laughed happily. They were sitting on a bench near The Lake in Central Park, not far from the little boat house.

Earlier, they had gone to a bakery and picked up coffee and croissants. It was a beautiful, late-June morning—the temperature was a perfect seventy-five degrees. A couple of joggers ran along the nearby path, and two young boys were getting ready to go out on the lake in a rowboat.

Jed took a long sip of his coffee. "What would you like to do today?"

"Umm—I don't know." Caitlin looked over at him, studying his handsome face. She noticed he was already acquiring his summer tan. There was a band of lighter skin across the top of his brow that his Stetson usually covered. "Can't we just stay here all day?" Caitlin asked, stretching luxuriously.

"Absolutely not!" Jed replied in mock outrage. "Some tour guide you are. You show me the park and that's it?" he cried, doing his best not to burst out laughing.

"Okay, you want to play tourist, we'll play tourist," Caitlin replied playfully. "Let's see—first we'll go out to Liberty Island and see the Statue, then we can visit the top of the World Trade Center. After that, we'll walk through TriBeCa and up through Greenwich Village." She stopped. "Or maybe we should go to South Street Seaport first, and then over to the Village."

"Enough, enough." Jed pulled her to her feet. "Come on. Let's go see what kind of trouble you're going to get me into." Giggling, Caitlin gave Jed a quick kiss, and then she ran off toward the road that led out of the park.

They spent a wonderful morning together, visiting tourist attractions and snapping pictures of each other with Jed's camera. They ate lunch at a charming Italian restaurant on Mulberry Street in the area known as Little Italy. Caitlin had started with tomato and mozzarella vinaigrette, then moved on to threadlike linguine, which tasted faintly of basil. Dessert was a vanilla custard that melted on her tongue. With a contented sigh, Caitlin put down her spoon after having gotten the last little bit at the bottom of her dish. "That was wonderful."

"It was," Jed agreed. "We'll have to remember to come back when I move here."

Caitlin nodded, happy for the moment. "I hope that'll be soon."

"I do, too. And speaking of that," Jed said, putting his napkin on the table, "I want to ask you something."

"Oh?" Caitlin asked, concerned because Jed suddenly seemed so serious.

"Well, since you haven't found an apartment yet, and since I'll be moving here as soon as

51

everything at the ranch is settled"—he looked into her eyes—"What would you think about us living together? I could get an apartment big enough for both of us. You could move in now."

"Uh—" Totally thrown, Caitlin didn't know what to say. "What about Melanie?" she said, asking the first question that occurred to her.

"She'd find her own apartment, I suppose." He rushed on. "She's only a year younger than us, you know. She'll be fine on her own."

"I know she will," Caitlin replied in a soft voice.

"We could live anywhere you want—the Village, maybe the Upper West Side. I wouldn't get anything you didn't like—you could even pick it out." Jed looked at her with an almost pleading expression. A moment earlier he had been so enthusiastic and excited, and Caitlin knew she was disappointing him. She looked down at her plate, at the traces of her dessert.

"Caitlin," Jed began again, "I thought this was something we've always wanted. I know I've wanted it."

"Yes, Jed, that's true," she said, looking up at him. "It's just that I wasn't expecting you to want to live together so soon." She gave him a tiny smile and reached across the table to take his hand. "This is a big decision, Jed, and I want to do the right thing—for both of us. Would you mind if I took a little while to think about it? Just for the rest of the weekend," she hurried to add, seeing the effect she was having on him. "You know I love you, Jed," she assured him softly.

"That's exactly why I thought you'd be excited about living with me." His voice turned cool. "I guess I was wrong."

"Jed, that's not fair. I just want some time to think, that's all." He was twisting the meaning of her words, and she hated it when someone did that—especially Jed. "Please! Try to understand," she cried a little too sharply.

"Caitlin, I'm sorry," Jed apologized. "I didn't mean to upset you. Look, take all the time you need to think it over." He forced himself to smile, but it wasn't easy.

For the rest of the day neither of them said a word about Jed's idea, but it was obvious that it weighed heavily on both their minds. Even the horse and carriage ride through Central Park, which should have been so romantic, couldn't keep Caitlin's mind off the decision she would have to make.

In bed that night she tossed and turned until her covers were hopelessly tangled. Finally she got up and went to the window. Leaning against the frame, she looked out into the night. The building across the street was low enough so that she could see the skyscrapers, which were dotted with white where lights had been left on. She did love Jed, she thought, so much that the thought of spending her life without him was devastating. Her decision, then, should have been easy—she should have just said yes right away.

But Caitlin had more to consider than just her feelings for Jed. Now, for the first time in her life, she had the freedom to make her own decisions, to be completely on her own. Her grandmother wasn't there to tell her what to do, how to act, and what to think. And Caitlin liked the feeling of independence. But, she reasoned, if she moved in with Jed some of that would change. He would want a say in what she did, where she went—even how she decorated the apartment. Caitlin knew she wasn't ready for that yet. She was also sure, however, that she would want to share her life with Jed—someday. And having waited to live together would make that day even more special.

When Caitlin told Jed of her decision at dinner on Sunday, he was terribly disappointed. "I understand, I guess," he had said. "You have to do what you think is right." But she knew he didn't really understand. Even after she had explained her reasons for wanting a place of her own a dozen times, he still just looked hurt and confused.

They were sitting in a restaurant near the apartment of Jed's friend, where he had stayed. They had just finished eating dinner and were waiting until it was time to leave for the airport.

"I hope you do understand. I'm not doing this to hurt you, you know," Caitlin desperately wished that somehow Jed would suddenly smile and nod his head and everything would be all right between them again.

"I said I understood," he assured her. But his voice was flat, emotionless.

"Okay," she said, telling herself to drop the subject. "Are you sure you didn't forget anything?" She asked the question, knowing it was the kind of thing people say when it's getting close to time to say goodbye and they've run out of normal conversation.

"Yeah, I'm sure." Jed glanced at his watch. "Well, I think I'd better go. I don't want to miss my flight." He stood up, picking up his overnight bag. Caitlin stood, too, and they walked out of the restaurant.

"Are you sure you don't want me to ride out to the airport with you?" she asked as they stepped out into the humid evening.

"No," Jed replied quickly. "It's a long ride, and it would be pointless for you to come, too." He scowled. "I didn't mean that to sound the way it did. I just meant that you shouldn't have to spend all that time in a cab when we've just had the weekend together and said our goodbyes." Before she could put up any further argument, he raised his hand to hail a cab. A moment later Caitlin was sitting in the backseat of a taxi and it was pulling away from the curb.

Twisting quickly, she watched while Jed climbed into his own cab. She wanted to have even that small last glimpse of him. As she stared, she felt a momentary stab of fear, almost as if the distance he was about to put between them was more than the physical one from New York to Montana.

But as she turned to face foward again, she told herself that she was being silly. Perhaps it was his father's recent death that was making Jed so insensitive to her needs, but whatever it was, it wouldn't last. Jed was too levelheaded to let it last. He would probably even think things over while he was on the plane and realize how unreasonable he was being. She smiled to herself, confident she was right. He would probably call her in the morning and tell her she had been right. Of course he would. Jed loved her.

6

Monday and Tuesday went by, and Jed didn't call. By Wednesday, Caitlin had reached the point where she was having trouble concentrating on her work. Each time her phone rang, her heart would leap. But then she would answer it only to find out it was Arlene calling with a question, or someone calling back about information she had requested. And each time as she hung up, she would scold herself for getting her hopes up. Jed wouldn't call her at work—not unless it was terribly important. But then, wasn't their relationship important?

When Jed finally did call, it was late that night. And their conversation was far from satisfying. He'd sounded so closed off, as if he didn't really want to talk and had only called because it was expected of him. But he did say he was tired, so maybe that was it. After all, it was almost midnight in New York, so in Montana it was just about ten. That was late considering the fact that everyone at the ranch was up by five o'clock every morning. Caitlin made a point of not talking too long.

Getting ready for bed, she told herself that she would write him a nice letter in the morning to try to make up for their brief call. She'd ask him all kinds of questions about himself in the letter. Yes, that should make him feel better.

But the letter never got written. Having overslept, Caitlin dressed in a hurry and gulped down a glass of grapefruit juice before dashing off to work.

Jed called the next night, Thursday, again. This time he sounded more like himself, and they talked for ages. Caitlin was smiling happily to herself as she hung up. But then she thought back to the moment in their conversation when she told him about the apartment she had just leased. She hadn't expected Jed to be thrilled by the sudden reminder that they wouldn't be living together, and he wasn't. Still, she supposed, it could have been worse. He had tried to hide his emotions.

Caitlin's thoughts turned to her new apartment. She'd found it on her own, very easily. On Tuesday Caitlin had overheard two other tenants talking about someone who was moving out in less than a week.

When she and Gloria went down to check the place out, Caitlin was horrified by the shape it was in. The once white walls were scuffed and dirty, and the wall-to-wall carpeting was a horrible shade of brown. And without any furniture, it looked even smaller than Gloria and Morgan's apartment.

"Take it!" Gloria told her as they walked through the bedroom. "Every apartment looks this bad in the beginning. But look at what you're getting—it's an okay size, in a good neighborhood, and you'll have me and Morgan right upstairs. Besides, knowing you, you'll turn this place into something that should be in *Architectural Digest*."

Standing in the redecorated apartment three weeks later, Caitlin had to admit that Gloria had been right to talk her into taking it. She'd replaced the brown carpet with one of a medium peach color. She had had the walls painted in a lighter tone of the same shade of peach. A couch ran the length of one wall of the living room, with two chairs facing it. All three pieces were upholstered in the same heavy, nubby cotton. There was a generously sized, glass coffee table in front of the couch. A bowl of fresh flowers stood on top of the table, and several plump scatter pillows of pastel colors that echoed those of the flowers were placed invitingly on the couch and chairs. An original Impressionist painting hung over the couch, flanked on either side by gold-framed Renior etchings. They were housewarming presents to Caitlin from her grandmother.

Caitlin's bedroom was a feminine delight, done all in rose and white. Her antique brass bed was covered by a fluffy eiderdown comforter and heaped high with lace pillows. There was an antique white wicker rocking chair across the room. It had to have sat on some Victorian front porch in the 1890s. And—just because she'd fallen in love with it when she'd spotted it in the same shop where she'd found the chair—there was a dressing screen in one corner. It was strictly decorative and she had put a potted fern in a stand in front of it.

"You really ought to throw a party," Morgan told her the day she moved in. "A housewarming party."

"That sounds like fun," Caitlin replied. "I definitely will. But first," she added with a mischievous giggle, "I want to have a sort of private housewarming with a certain person."

"Jed?"

"Um-hmm." Caitlin's eyes got a faraway happy look. "He'll be here soon."

"I hate to throw cold water on that dreamy look you have, but is that such a good idea? I mean, after all, he did want you to live with him. Wouldn't you kind of be rubbing it in?"

"I'm not worried," Caitlin told her. "Actually, when I talked to him last night, he sounded genuinely interested in how I'd decorated the place."

"Really?" Morgan remarked in a surprised tone. "Well, that's a good sign."

"In fact, he just found a place of his own," Caitlin said, walking over to straighten a pillow on the couch. "It's a two-bedroom over on West Seventy-sixth. Of course he hasn't seen it yet, since he dealt with the broker by phone, but from the description, it sounds great. Huge windows in the living room that look out on the Hudson River, a real dining room, and—get this—a working fireplace."

"Wow! Sounds impressive."

"Well, he needs a big place. It's going to be his only home, and he's having a fair amount of furniture shipped here from the ranch. And those kind of things would hardly fit into a place the size of this one."

"It sounds like he's going to bring a little bit of the West to New York," Morgan mused. "Aren't you a little worried that he'll get here and hate it, and then he'll want to go back home?"

"Not really," Caitlin replied with a light laugh. Morgan could be too much sometimes. "Don't you have a dinner date? It's almost six-thirty."

"Oh, my gosh!" Jed totally forgotten, Morgan glanced at her watch. "I've got to dash if I'm going to take a shower and be ready in an hour," she cried, heading for the door. "Well, enjoy your new place." She smiled. "I know I would."

The sound of the elevator door shutting down the hall told Caitlin she was, at last, alone in her totally finished apartment. To celebrate the occasion, she went into the kitchen and took out the tiny split of champagne Arlene had given her as a housewarming gift. A moment later, having toasted her new independence, she went into the bedroom. With a wry smile, she stared at the clothes on the bed and chair that still had to be put away. Setting her glass down on the curlicued wicker bed table, she grabbed up several padded hangers and headed for the closet. At least now she had a closet all to herself.

A few weeks later Caitlin, chic in a pale yellow linen top and long pleated skirt, rushed back into the *National News* building after spending her lunch hour shopping. Despite the oppressive August heat that shimmered on the streets outside, she looked cool and together.

"You're incredible," Arlene said as she followed Caitlin to the door of her office. She leaned against the door frame and watched as Caitlin slid into her chair, put her purse away in the bottom drawer of her desk, and set the shopping bag she was carrying on the top of the bookcase. "How come you still look so polished after being out in that awful heat?" She pushed a strand of auburn hair into the twist at the back of her head. "All I did was walk across the street to pick up a sandwich and I absolutely fell apart." She looked critically at her rumpled skirt. "Look at me! I'm a mess."

"You are not," Caitlin assured her with a warm smile. "In fact, I was just thinking how cool and collected you look, too."

"I can always hope. Anyway, there's a lot going on this afternoon, so why don't you come into my office as soon as you get settled." She was just about to leave when she noticed the shopping bag again. "Oh, did you find a Welcome-To-New-York present for Jed?"

"Yes. Oh, Arlene, I got him the most marvelous—"

Just then the phone rang, interrupting her. She reached for it, and after saying hello, handed it to Arlene. "For you—it's Sterling."

Their conversation was brief, but as they spoke, Arlene's features changed from relaxed to all business. She hung up and said, "I've got to go. If anyone wants me, tell them I'm in a meeting with Sterling and we're not to be disturbed." Arlene turned and started to head down the hall toward the editor-in-chief's office.

Then she came back. "Oh, Caitlin, the reason I followed you in here was to remind you that the photo session for that article on young professional women is set for tomorrow morning. It seems they need the cover shot right away." She paused, a slight scowl creasing her forehead. "You're just about finished with the copy for that, aren't you?"

"Yes," Caitlin assured her, nodding. "Down to the last fact. All I have to do is retype it. You know, I got really involved in that article."

"I thought you would. That's why I got you involved—I thought the subject would be right up your alley. Oops, I seem to be talking in clichés this afternoon. Bad sign for an editor." She grimaced. "Comes from trying to do too much, which is exactly why I want you at that shoot. I need you to take some of the pressure off me."

"I'll be there first thing," Caitlin promised.

"Terrific, because there's—"

The phone rang again, cutting her off. Caitlin reached for it.

"If that's Sterling, tell him I'm out of here," Arlene whispered, already stepping back into the hall. Caitlin covered the receiver with her hand, and Arlene added, "Oh, and have a good time with Jed tonight. But not too good a time, okay?" she warned. "I don't want you tired tomorrow morning when I need you to be sharp." Then she was gone.

The phone call had indeed been Sterling Drummond, the editor-in-chief and Arlene's boss. Caitlin told a white lie, saying Arlene had left her office several minutes before and that she should be there any second. She smiled, thinking, *Poor Arlene, always on the run.* She also wondered if she'd be that way in a year or two. But, no, she thought as she rolled a fresh sheet of paper into her typewriter. Caitlin wanted to be a writer, not an editor. She smiled. Yes, that was her goal—to become the best magazine writer she could be—maybe she'd even win a Pulitzer prize. She laughed at herself as she started typing the first line. *Well, why not,* she argued back. *Whoever got anywhere by thinking small?*

Caitlin hurried home after work and headed straight for the kitchen, where she unpacked the groceries she'd bought on her way from the office. Then she hopped into the shower. Letting the water run over her, she went over the menu she'd planned. She would serve thin slices of cold roast beef with Dijon mustard sauce, little red new potatoes, a crispy green salad, and hot dinner rolls straight from the oven.

Later, dressed in white silk hostess pajamas, with her hair pinned up, she went back into the kitchen again. After turning the oven on to warm, she took out the rolls she'd bought at a nearby bakery and placed them on a cookie sheet. Then she got out the salad makings.

By the time Jed arrived, the yeasty aroma of baking rolls had filled the apartment. "Umm," he said, pulling Caitlin into his arms, "something certainly smells good. And so do you," he added, nuzzling her neck where she had sprayed some of her favorite perfume—Chanel No. 5.

Kissing him back warmly, Caitlin wrapped her arms around his neck. She always felt so secure, so protected in Jed's arms. Then, suddenly she remembered the rolls and had to break away and dash to the kitchen before they burned.

Jed followed her and leaned casually against the door frame observing her. Finally Caitlin pressed him into service, asking him to uncork the chilled white wine while she put the final touches on the salad.

She had already set a table for two in the living room with crystal and silver and white candles. She lit the candles, and Jed helped carry in the food, then held her chair while she sat down. After taking the seat across from her, he picked up his glass of wine and toasted her. His eyes were warm and full of love as he said, "Here's to the most beautiful and talented girl in the world." Glancing down at the sumptuous feast before him, a confused look came over his face, and he added, "And the best cook." He took a sip and then put his glass down again. "When did you learn how to make all this? I can hardly believe it. And from a girl who grew up in a household with a full-time cook, too. I certainly don't remember your doing anything like this during college." He shook his head. "Sand-wiches from the deli, yes, but—" He took a bite of the roast beef. "This is delicious."

"Now I feel terrible," Caitlin said with a guilty laugh. "I got most of this stuff at the deli on Third Avenue. I was hoping you'd think just exactly what you did—that I'd turned into a fabulous cook over the past few weeks."

"Well, all I can say is that you can fix deli food for me any day." He reached across the table to take her hand and squeeze it. "Just as long as you're there to eat it with me."

The rest of dinner went by quickly. Jed filled Caitlin in on how Melanie was, and then Caitlin told him about some of the new friends she'd made, and the restaurants she'd discovered. "I've been going out to lunch a lot and even to a couple of plays," she said. "Oh, Jed, there are so many places I want to show you."

Later after they cleared away the dishes, Caitlin made iced cappuccino, which they took into the living room. While Jed took a seat on the couch, Caitlin went into her bedroom and got the copy of the article about young working women that she'd worked on for Arlene. Proudly she handed the neatly typed pages to him, then sat down beside him. "This is what I've been working on for the past few weeks," she said, picking up her drink. She sipped it quietly as he started to read.

Caitlin watched as a look of surprise came over Jed's face. She could hardly wait to hear what he would say when he finished reading. Finally he put the pages down.

"This is great, really great," he said. With a shake of his head, he looked at her. "Caitlin, when did you start doing this sort of thing? When we talked on the phone you never mentioned anything about writing." He looked angry.

"Well, I didn't exactly write the whole thing," she explained. "The author, her name is Jolie King—Jed, you'd love her," Caitlin interrupted herself. "She's just terrific. Anyway, Jolie asked me if I'd like to help her out a little on the research. Once I'd done that, she let me write some of it, that's all."

"You didn't tell me any of this," he insisted. "And I would have thought you would. This is important—this piece." He tapped a finger on the pages. "You've obviously been working on this for some time, but you didn't once think to mention it. If I were involved in something this important, I would have told you." Caitlin suddenly realized that Jed sounded more hurt than angry. Jed went on. "What else haven't you told me? And what about all those new friends you were talking—"

"Jed," Caitlin broke in, "I didn't mention these things because I didn't think you'd be interested. You were in Montana, and, well, I just didn't want to go on and on about having a good time while you were so wrapped up in turning the ranch over to those investors."

"I'm sorry, Caitlin," Jed answered, looking slightly sheepish. "I guess I was just feeling sorry for myself. These last few weeks have been so awful. I guess I just feel like I don't *belong* anywhere, anymore."

Caitlin didn't reply, but instead leaned over and kissed him lightly on the lips. "You know what you need? You need to get out, to discover the city. Once everything starts to seem more familiar, you'll feel right at home. Honest, that's exactly what happened to me. In fact, that's why I got you what I did—" She stopped in midsentence, puting her hand to her mouth. "Oh, my gosh, I completely forgot about the present I bought for you."

"A present?" Jed asked, looking a little confused. "For me?"

"Of course it's for you, dummy. Who else would it be for?" Jed just smiled helplessly and shrugged, and Caitlin suddenly felt much better. Certain that Jed's moment of self-pity had passed, she jumped up and hurried across the room to the wall unit that not only held her books and stereo, but had a small storage compartment as well. Opening the door, she took out a small white box tied up with a red bow and walked back over to the couch. She handed the box to Jed, then sat down next to him and watched as he untied the ribbon and lifted the lid.

Inside he found a small book that was bound in soft, dark green leather. A thin gold border had been embossed on the front, and Jed's initials—J.S.M.—were printed on the bottom righthand corner. "Caitlin, this is beautiful," Jed whispered as he lifted the book out of the box.

"You'll never guess what it is," Caitlin called out happily. "It's not an appointment book or an address book," she added mysteriously.

"Then what is it?"

"It's an *everything* book," she replied. Moving closer to him, she reached over and opened the book, which he was holding in his lap. "See, there's a place for you to make notes, and here's some graph paper, and there's even a few slots for credit cards and stuff. But the best part—the reason I got it for you—is that this one comes with a New York street and subway map, as well as an entertainment guide to the city. See, now you'll learn your way around in no time." She cupped her hand over his knee. "I saw it and I just had to get it for you."

"Well, I love it," he said as he leaned over and kissed her. "And I'm going to make good use of it. You wait and see."

"Look," she said, flipping to the map again. "I even marked all the places we went that weekend you were here." She turned to him, her eyes dancing. "Remember how much fun we had." She didn't, however, mention the tense way that weekend had ended. Instead she reached up and ran a finger lightly along the strong line of his jaw. "Oh, Jed, you really are going to fall in love with New York."

"I don't know if I've got room for New York," Jed said, his voice warm and low. "Considering my love for you, there's no room for anything, or anyone else."

"Oh, Jed, I do love you," she whispered softly as she looked deep into his eyes. "I'm so glad you're finally here. Let's promise that we'll never let ourselves be separated again."

"Agreed," Jed said. "Absolutely." Then Jed took Caitlin into his arms, kissed her gently. She melted against him, and he kissed her again, this time with all the fierceness of his love for her.

Finally he broke away. "We'll never be separated again," he said, his voice husky. "For any reason."

7

As Caitlin walked through the doors of the *National News* building the following morning, she felt as though she were walking on clouds. She could think of nothing but Jed—she could almost feel the strength of his arms around her as he'd held her and the pressure of his mouth against hers as he'd kissed her. She smiled to herself as she stepped into the elevator and pushed the button for the thirty-sixth floor.

As the elevator began to climb, however, Caitlin made herself concentrate on her job, and the people she would be working with during the morning photography session.

Arlene had told Caitlin that Peter Leonard would be the photographer. At thirty-four, he already had a wonderful reputation for his ability to bring out his subject's true beauty, both inner and physical. He wasn't on *National*'s staff, but he did at least ninety percent of their portrait covers.

Caitlin had met Peter the previous week in Arlene's office. His smile and open friendliness had made her like him right away. She decided that he wasn't as ruggedly handsome as Jed, but he did have an all-American attractiveness about him. From the outdoor location work he did, his lean face was nearly as deeply tanned as Jed's. And while he was dressed casually in loafers, jeans, and a loose cotton sweater, he had an air of sophistication that made it easy for Caitlin to imagine him looking equally at ease in a dinner jacket. His eyes were an interesting shade of grayish brown, and his sandy hair fell almost to his shoulders. Peter's voice, as he'd held out his hand to say hello, was warm, echoing his friendly manner.

There was no trace of that warmth, however, when she heard Peter's voice raised as she stepped off of the elevator.

"All right, then, just what the hell do you suggest we do?" Peter demanded. His words could be heard clearly through the heavy swinging doors that led from the hall into the spacious studio.

Caitlin's heart began to pound. What could have happened to make him so mad so early in the morning, she wondered. Then she heard

Arlene's voice. It was almost a whisper, though, so Caitlin couldn't make out what she was saying. Crossing the hall, she pushed one of the doors open and stepped into the room.

Arlene and Peter were standing facing each other about ten feet from the door, but neither of them saw her come in. They were totally engrossed in whatever they were arguing about. Actually, Caitlin discovered, Peter was the one who was angry; Arlene was only trying to calm him down.

"Well, since I can't shoot her, just who am I supposed to photograph?" he shouted again, waving his arm in the direction of the empty, unlit set.

"This is not the time to get hysterical, Peter," Arlene said in a flat tone. "We'll figure something out. Artie is in the back making a pot of strong coffee; maybe that'll help."

"Ten gallons of coffee wouldn't sober that girl up," someone called from across the room. Caitlin turned to Jolie King, the author, who was walking over to where Peter and Arlene were standing. She was a short, slightly overweight woman of about forty with a look of directness. "You know, I just don't believe it, Arlene," she added, shaking her head. "I interviewed more than a dozen women who could have been featured on the cover, and you picked the one idiot who would go and get herself drunk before a morning shoot. Terrific! Just terrific."

"Jolie," Arlene replied, "I can understand that you're upset, but may I remind you that you approved my decision to use this girl. And I, for one, would choose her again. She has the perfect look for the cover. It's just that, well— you certainly can't fault me for not bothering to ask her if she would make sure and be sober for a nine A.M. shoot."

"No, I suppose not," Jolie conceded. "But if you'd listened to me—"

"Look," Peter shouted, raising his voice in order to get their attention, "you can both keep right on arguing about who's responsible, but we've got work to do. Am I going to have someone to shoot, or not?"

"All right, fine!" Jolie threw up her hands in disgust. "We'll get you a new model, and I'll rewrite the whole article to fit her in," she said raging. Then suddenly she turned and looked at Caitlin. Waving a hand in her direction, she asked, "What about one of the girls Caitlin interviewed for me? Caitlin, wasn't one of them your roommate? Could you call her and have her come down here?"

"Forget it," Peter said. "There isn't time."

"What do you mean there's no time?" Jolie countered with a scowl at Peter. "What difference will a couple of hours make?"

"I'm supposed to be across town for another assignment at noon. That'll take the rest of the day and maybe into tomorrow. I suppose I could make time first thing Thursday if I had to."

"How about it? Can't we wait?" Jolie inquired, turning to face Arlene.

"No," Arlene answered, "we can't wait past today. The article was pushed up to fill the place of that one that fell through about surrogate mothers."

"Great!" Jolie cried. "Tell me, do *you* have any suggestions?"

Arlene let out an unhappy sigh. "Not right now, no. But let me think."

Suddenly Peter let out a loud whoop. "I've got it!" he shouted, grinning. "I've got the perfect solution. Why didn't any of us think of her before? It's so obvious."

"What is?" Arlene asked, looking absolutely mystified.

"Caitlin!" Peter announced. Practically sprinting to Caitlin's side, he put an arm around her shoulders. "She's perfect for the cover shot. I mean, you couldn't ask for a better example of a young, professional woman on her own, now could you?" He looked from Arlene to Jolie, then back to Arlene again. "What do you think?"

"But she's not one of the young women we interviewed for the article," Jolie insisted before Arlene could answer.

"Even better," Peter argued. "You just said she did some of the interviewing. As far as I'm concerned, that's involved."

"Well—" Jolie frowned thoughtfully.

"You're absolutely right, Peter!" Arlene exclaimed. "She'll be okay."

"Not just okay," Peter said quietly as he looked directly at Caitlin. "She'll be perfect."

8

Jed's classes at Columbia began the first week in September. Melanie, sitting at the dining room table eating breakfast, watched as Jed left for his first day at law school. Her own classes at NYU—which she had gotten into at the last minute—didn't start for another two weeks. As Jed closed the door behind him, she knew she couldn't spend a long, boring day hanging around the apartment by herself. She was going out exploring.

True, she had already gone sightseeing with Jed. But she found the places they'd visited— Wall Street, Liberty Island, Lincoln Center, and a couple of musty museums—incredibly dull. In fact, they had bored her stiff. She wanted to see the real city, the one Caitlin had talked about. She remembered the week before when Caitlin had invited her to lunch and talked about New York with so much enthusiasm. She had even suggested to Melanie that they go down to the Village that afternoon and walk around NYU for a while. Melanie wanted to go, but she had already made an appointment to have her hair cut. *That's where I'll go today*, Melanie thought as she stood up and brought her cereal bowl into the kitchen, *down to NYU*.

Stepping off the bus at the foot of Fifth Avenue, Melanie paused at the edge of the sidewalk to get her bearings. Dressed in an oversize, cotton knit sweater, a pair of navy tights, and black flats, she hoped she looked as though she belonged. Already she was beginning to hate the idea that anyone would mistake her for an out-of-towner. As the crowds of people surged past her without so much as a raised eyebrow, she decided her outfit was fine. She was being totally ignored and that, as far as Melanie was concerned, was a good sign. She had firmly decided—after making up her mind to move to New York—that she was leaving her western life completely behind her.

Washington Square Park was directly in front of her, just across the street. Watching the traffic, she stepped off the curb and began to cross the street. She remembered some phrases in one of her NYU brochures describing the park. "All the streets centered around the park. . . . It was the focal point of the Village. . . . Originally it had been just an open public place where executions had taken place in the 1700s and where poor people had sometimes been buried. Now a fountain stood on the spot where the bones of over ten thousand unknown people lay buried. . . ."

A shiver ran down her spine in spite of the warm late-summer weather. Dead people . . . bones rotting in the ground . . . death . . . her father. Thoughts of him would pop into her mind at the oddest times. When was she going to get through a day without thinking about him? she wondered.

Melanie noticed that a street musician and a mime were working the area around the fountain. A small crowd of people had stopped to listen and watch.

Pushing thoughts of her father from her mind, Melanie walked toward the musician, stopping next to a couple with their arms around each other's waists. The man, standing with the fountain as a backdrop, was playing a guitar. He wasn't paying any attention to the people watching him, concentrating instead on his music. Melanie thought he was good-looking in a sensitive way. His face had a kind of poetic anger to it. Suddenly he looked up at her as if he had known that she was staring at him. Embarrassed, she turned away, but not before fishing in her pocket for some change and dropping it into his guitar case.

She was still thinking about her brief encounter as she approached the corner of Washington Square South and LaGuardia Place.

"Watch it!" a strong male voice called, stopping her just as she was about to step off a curb.

"Huh?" She looked around in confusion and noticed a tall boy about her own age glaring down at her. He had short, spiky hair and was wearing a tank top and baggy cotton pants. Melanie noticed he had a thin gold wire hoop in his ear.

"You were about to walk in front of that cab, you know." He flicked his head at the battered yellow car now halfway up the next block.

"Oh!" Melanie exclaimed, embarrassed. How dumb, she thought. She was acting like a hick after all, not watching where she was going. "Well, I'm fine now."

"I guess you are," he answered, an amused smile turning up the corners of his mouth. "Tell me, do you always walk out into oncoming traffic, or was it my amazing looks that made you lose your head?"

"Neither," she mumbled. "I just didn't see." The light changed to green, and she started across the street.

"Hey, wait," he called, catching up to her. On the other side of the street, Melanie continued walking, heading for LaGuardia Place.

He kept on walking right beside her. "You go to NYU?"

She nodded, not looking at him.

"So you're a student," he remarked. This time she gave him the slightest glance as she nodded. "So am I," he said.

They kept walking for another block before he spoke again. "Look, I don't usually do this, but do you want to go for coffee or something?"

This time when she looked around he gave her a slow, lazy grin. "There's a great coffee shop not far from here."

"I—I—"

"We could go somewhere else, if you'd rather." His voice made it clear that he was finding her reaction to him amusing. "Look, I really don't bite," he added and smiled again. "And I'd really like to get to know you. You look like a nice person. But if you would prefer to just walk away right now, I can't stop you." He stopped and gave her a incredibly hurt look.

Melanie couldn't help laughing. And as she did, she thought to herself that he was really cute. "Just coffee?"

"Just plain coffee," he promised.

"All right," she said, nodding. "Sure."

* * *

Two hours later as she sat across from the boy, whose name was Cole Hillerman, she had to stop herself from grinning. She was having her first real adventure in New York—with a guy wearing a single earring and his hair cut punk. What would her friends back in Montana think if they could see her now? For that matter, what would Jed say? He would probably throw a fit, that's what, she thought, nearly giggling at the idea.

"So, Mel, do you want to go to the rock concert Friday night?" Cole was asking when she turned her attention back to him.

"Sure," she answered quickly. She thought for a second. "Do you mind if I meet you there?" she asked, thinking that she could then tell Jed that she was going to a movie with a girl she'd met. She smiled at Cole. "That way you won't have to come all the way uptown." There was no reason why Jed and Cole should have to meet right away—no reason to give him the chance to disapprove. She sighed. Jed was just so old-fashioned sometimes. You'd think he was her father, not a brother who was only a year older. "Is that okay with you?" she asked Cole.

"That's perfect, Mel. I'll be looking forward to it."

Melanie smiled happily as they left the coffee shop.

As first, Jed threw himself into his studies at Columbia, sometimes hitting the books until two or three in the morning. He would drill himself until he could answer nearly any question an instructor might ask him.

But no matter how engrossed he was in his classes, he always made time to call Caitlin, to talk to her about her day and to tell her how much he loved her. He would sit at his desk, the phone against his ear, looking at the framed photo that sat in front of him, and wish that he were holding her in his arms instead of speaking to her over a distance of half the city.

Sometimes he hated it that both of their lives had taken on such a hectic pace. He missed the days when they were in college and saw each other every day.

As September wore on, Jed began feeling more and more unsure that living in New York and studying law were what he really wanted. After all, where would all the years of hard work he would have to put in get him? What had hard work gotten his father except an early grave and an ungrateful son? In his heart, Jed knew he hadn't been ungrateful, and his father had been happy; he had liked his life. But somehow, the guilt ate at Jed, anyway. He began to have trouble concentrating on his classes. It was easy enough to cut the ones that no longer interested him, though. Who would ever know? As long as he could pass his finals, why worry? And finals were months away.

One morning, after a restless night filled with uneasy dreams of the ranch and his father, Jed went to a class he hadn't been to in a week. He sat in the lecture hall not paying the slightest attention. At the end of the hour Bill Strang, a classmate he'd talked with a few times, came over and asked Jed if he'd like to join him at the Law Library for lunch. The Law Library was a pub only a few blocks away, and it served delicious deli sandwiches.

"You look like you could use a break," Bill said with a knowing grin. "A bunch of us are going over there, and you're welcome to join us if you want."

"Sounds great," Jed said, accepting the invitation. Scooping up his books, he followed Bill out of the lecture hall.

Half an hour later Jed was sitting in a large booth at the Library with a group of guys he'd seen in class but never met before. They seemed nice enough, and Jed allowed himself the luxury of relaxing a little. It felt good.

"Hey, Jed!" Chip Mason called from across the table, rapping on the surface to get Jed's attention. Chip was a second year student whose father was a senior partner in one of the largest law firms in the city. "Are you still with us?"

Puzzled, Jed stared back at him. Obviously he'd missed something that Chip had said. "What?"

"I asked if you wanted to come sailing with us. It's way too nice a day to waste on law." He motioned toward a tall, brown-haired boy slumped at the end of the booth. "Griffith's father has a boat that's just aching for us to take her out," he explained. "His dad's taking her out of the water tomorrow so this is our last chance. Do you want to go?"

Jed shrugged. "Sure, why not?"

Hours later, relaxing on the deck of the sleek sailboat as it moved smoothly across the bright waters of Long Island Sound, Jed leaned back and closed his eyes. The sun was wonderfully warm on his shoulders and the air smelled so good—fresh and salty, both at the same time.

He listened to the sounds of the other guys talking and laughing. He liked them. Bill, Chip, and Griffith were great guys, and it felt good to have friends again. As for missing class that afternoon, he would just have to hit the books extra hard that night. But then Jed remembered that Chip had said something about going out that night, going to some club. Well, what was another night of not studying, anyway? There was plenty of time to study—plenty of time.

Jed wasn't the only one who had been missing classes. Melanie had been playing hooky fairly often as well. It had taken her only a week of sitting in stuffy classrooms to realize she was not exactly thrilled with what she was doing. Somehow studying the history of radio and television didn't seem to have much to do with what was happening in the real world.

Cole, on the other hand, *was* the real world. He believed that the only way to know what was important in life was to experience everything firsthand. Together they sat for hours in coffee shops discussing art and life with Cole's friends. Melanie didn't always understand everything they said, and Cole even yelled at her occasionally for saying things he thought were ignorant. But he would always apologize, and Melanie never stayed hurt for long.

Caitlin, meanwhile, was completely unaware of what was going on with either Jed or Melanie. Arlene had started giving her more and more small writing assignments, and because they were in addition to her regular job, she worked a lot in the evenings at home. She still called Jed on the phone most evenings. Sometimes he wouldn't be there, though.

Caitlin started to wonder how Jed could go out so often, but he explained, saying he had joined a study group. But then, when she would ask him how his studies were going, he would change the subject. Caitlin wasn't sure what was going on, but what could she do? She couldn't accuse him of not keeping up with his work because she didn't know that he wasn't. Besides, she reasoned, Jed wouldn't do anything to jeopardize his standing at Columbia. Or would he?

But then on the last weekend in September, something happened that forced Caitlin to recognize the fact that things really might be going wrong for Jed. Jed had taken her dancing at one of the trendiest new clubs in the city. She had never been there before and assumed that Jed hadn't, either. After all, he wouldn't have gone there without her.

They had just arrived and were standing in the lobby when two guys about their age came in. One of them, the taller of the pair, seemed to recognize Jed. When Caitlin turned toward Jed to ask if they were friends, she saw Jed's face turn red. "Let's get out of here," he muttered.

But it was too late. The guy was already weaving his way over to them. Moments later he flung his arm around Jed's shoulders. "Hey, old buddy," he said in a loud voice, "you're really getting to like this place, aren't you?" Then, before Jed could say a word, the young man swiveled to stare at Caitlin. "Hi, gorgeous. And how are you this lovely evening?" he asked expansively.

"Just fine," Caitlin replied in a cold voice. The young man smiled and stumbled back over to his friends.

As soon as they were alone again, Jed insisted they leave and go someplace else. Caitlin agreed, deciding not to say anything until later in the evening. Then, when she questioned Jed, he tried to make light of the incident. He explained that the guy had obviously mistaken him for someone else. Caitlin knew he was lying.

Later that night alone in her apartment, Caitlin sat in her darkened bedroom, worrying about Jed. What was happening to him? As she tossed and turned, she began to wonder how many of those nights he'd told her he was studying were really spent going out to clubs. And she wondered if that obnoxious young man they'd seen was a good friend of Jed's. Maybe he was just someone Jed knew casually. She hated to think of Jed drinking and staying out late. Why would he? How could he possibly risk flunking out of Columbia? He wasn't the same since his father had died. The smart, determined, dependable person she had fallen in love with was being replaced by a careless young man with the ambition of a pea.

Could it be possible, she wondered, that Jed was acting this way and hiding it from her because he was still feeling guilty about his father's death? Was he still punishing himself for not wanting to run the ranch? As she thought about it, it was the only explanation that made sense. It even explained the way Jed was risking his law career. *Oh, Jed, Jed, Jed,* she cried silently. *How could you? How could you do this to yourself?* Finally, near dawn, she fell into an exhausted sleep. But she also promised herself that she would find time in the next few days to have a talk with Jed. Somehow, she would find a way to help him.

9

"Caitlin, do you have a minute?" Peter Leonard asked as he leaned into Caitlin's cubicle, one hand on the partition. "Caitlin? Hey, Caitlin!" He shook her shoulder.

"Uh—oh, hi, Peter!" Caitlin replied, looking up distractedly from the page she was supposed to be proofreading. Actually, her mind had been on Jed and her decision of the night before to talk to him. She felt tired. "Sorry, I guess I was lost in thought."

"Must be interesting stuff," he commented wryly, nodding toward her desk and the pile of galley pages.

"Only if you're a sea lion," she countered with a smile. "This article is about—oh, never mind. Just take it from me, it's not that fascinating."

"Well, I think I've got something that you will

find interesting," he said, mysteriously. "So, if you've got a minute, can I lure you down to my darkroom?"

"Peter!" Caitlin pretended to be prudishly offended. "What kind of a line is that?"

"Whatever you want it to be," Peter said, joking. "Now quit trying to spar with the master of the innuendo, and come on."

"Okay, I'm yours." Throwing her pencil down on her desk, Caitlin stood up. "And don't you dare take that the wrong way," she said, laughing. She followed him down the hall toward the elevator. "What did you want to show me?"

But Peter insisted on keeping it a secret during the ride to the floor below and as they walked through the huge, vacant studio. Throwing open the door to the darkroom, which was lit with a single overhead bulb, he showed her over to the corner. "Ta-da!"

In front of her, propped on the tiled surface of a work table, was the mock-up of the next week's cover.

Smiling back at Caitlin was her own face just below the red and white *National News* banner and familiar logo. For a moment she was speechless. The cover looked so—so official. For the very first time she realized that her face was actually going to be seen on the cover of a magazine that would be sold not only across the

United States, but in several countries around the world.

"Well?" Peter asked after Caitlin had stared at it in silence for an unbearably long time. "Does that mean you like it or not? And if you don't like it, I will never forgive you." He looked at her expectantly.

"I'm not sure what to say," she replied at last. "It's sort of—overwhelming." She shook her head. "You're a wonderful photographer. I mean, you've made me look—beautiful."

He put his arms around her shoulders and squeezed her enthusiastically. "I think so, too," he admitted with a laugh. "Caitlin, you're one of those rare people who is not only fabulous looking in person, but you photograph that way, too."

"But, Peter—" she protested.

"But, nothing!" His eyes met hers. Then he looked back at the mock-up of the cover. "If I say so myself, that is the greatest-looking cover *National* has ever had." He hugged her again. "Just you wait. Next week, when this comes out, everyone will be talking about Caitlin Ryan, the new face in town."

"I'm famous," Morgan cried. She was sitting on Caitlin's couch, poring over her copy of *National News* with Caitlin's picture on the cover.

"You're famous?" Gloria asked, looking up from her own copy of *National*. "We're *all* famous!"

"Only for a week," Caitlin reminded them as she walked back into the living room from the kitchen. She was carrying a tray of ice-filled glasses of Diet Coke. Setting the tray down on the coffee table, she went on. "Next week, all of this fame will be forgotten."

"I don't care!" Morgan shrugged, throwing her head back and striking a model's pose. "This week it's total fame, and I love it!" She then pouted and said, "I just wish I'd gotten my picture taken for the article. Still, I do like the way I was written up. It made me seem kind of glamorous, don't you think?"

"Lest you forget, it was Caitlin who did that interview, Morgan," Gloria reminded her. She smiled at Caitlin. "It really is very good. I remember how hard you worked on it, and a lot of your style shows through."

"Thanks, Gloria," Caitlin said. "I really did work hard." Sitting on the couch, she picked up a glass and sipped at her Diet Coke. "As far as I'm concerned, my part in doing the article was much more interesting than the cover shot. After all, becoming a good writer is my real goal. Being on the cover was just a fluke. It wasn't as if I had to do anything special to be picked for it."

"Just be beautiful, that's all," Morgan said

wryly. She fell back against the couch. "I would have given my eyeteeth to be on a magazine cover."

"But if you did, no one would want to photograph you," Gloria cracked.

"Funny! Very funny!" Morgan wrinkled her nose at her roommate.

Caitlin laughed lightly. "Morgan, you can't say you didn't ask for it—"

The phone rang, interrupting her.

"A fan no doubt," Gloria said as Caitlin picked up the phone.

"Hello," Caitlin said. Then a second later she put her hand over the mouthpiece and whispered that it was Jed.

"Ah," Morgan said, giving Gloria a knowing look. Gloria started to stand. "We're leaving," she said, and grabbing Morgan's hand, she hauled her to her feet. "Come on, famous person, let's go back up to our own apartment. We can read our interviews aloud to each other."

That evening, dressed in a wide-shouldered knit dress that she'd cinched with a heavy, silver-buckled belt, Caitlin stood in front of her bathroom mirror putting the finishing touches on her makeup. Closing her lipstick, she dropped it into the silver mesh bag she intended to take with her to dinner. She had pinned her hair up, and a few tendrils curled softly on her neck. The diamond studs that her grandmother had given her for her twenty-first birthday the previous November were in her ears. She met the dark-fringed, deep blue eyes of her reflection and, with a sigh, decided that she was now glamorous enough for Jed's crowd. Picking up the silver bag, she made her way back through the bedroom and into the living room, sitting down on one of the white chairs to wait for Jed.

He had called that afternoon to say that his friends were dying to meet his glamorous girl-friend and had suggested dinner out. "How about Caramba?" He named one of the most popular Mexican restaurants in the city.

She'd hesitated. It was a week night, and she needed her sleep in order to be sharp at work the next day. She thought about Jed, too—about his classes. Guiltily, she remembered that she still hadn't found the chance to talk to him about his spending so many nights going out when he should be home hitting the books. Well, maybe tonight would be her chance. "I'd love to go, Jed." She'd paused. "Who else is going to be there?"

"Not too many people. Just some friends," he had told her. So now, there she was, dressed and ready to be taken out and presented to a group of people she really didn't feel the least bit like meeting. Well, she would be polite and answer the questions she knew would be put to her. Then after dinner, she'd explain that she had to make it an early night. Perhaps then she and Jed could come back to her apartment and have a talk. She glanced toward the small gold and glass clock on the end table. Eight thirty-five. She felt a flick of annoyance. Here she was hoping to make it an early evening, and Jed was late.

Three hours later Caitlin was checking the time again. Dinner had dragged on forever. There had been course after course, very little of which she had touched. And Jed's friends looked as if they were ready to go on partying for another several hours.

For a while Caitlin had been the center of conversation. Thankfully, they had moved on to other subjects. Now they were discussing the merits of various sailboats, and how fast each could go. Except for herself, they were all enjoying their second after-dinner drink. Caitlin was sipping a Perrier water and wishing that she were at home getting ready for bed. Her eyes felt tired and they burned from the cigarette smoke in their section of the restaurant. Twice in the past twenty minutes she had given Jed a look that said, "Let's go." Each time he had nodded, but then gotten involved in the conversation again. Finally, she had had enough.

"I'm sorry," she said, standing up. "But I've really got to leave." She put her hand on Jed's arm and looked at him sweetly.

"Oh, sure, I guess I'd better get you home," he said, finally getting her message.

As he stood up and helped Caitlin on with her coat, there was the usual chorus of goodbyes. They had started walking away from the table when Chip called after Jed, "We'll probably be going on to Max's from here if you want to try and catch up with us there."

Furious, Caitlin vowed not to say anything in front of Jed's friends that would embarrass him. She would be silent until they reached her place. But as the cab pulled away from the curb, and headed toward East Eighty-fourth Street, where she lived, Jed was still bubbling with excitement over Caitlin's current celebrity status. "You really wowed them back there. When you went to the ladies' room with Tina or whatever her name was, Chip said he thought you were dynamite. He even suggested we all go dancing down at Limelight tomorrow night. Doesn't that sound—"

"Jed, no!" Caitlin cried. It was too much for her. She had to say something. Ignoring the fact that the cab driver could hear every word she said, she turned in her seat and looked directly at Jed. "I'm not about to start living the kind of life you've obviously chosen, and I think you should think very seriously about where you're heading.

"You can't possibly tell me that you're keeping up at Columbia and going out every night." She shook her head violently. "I hate it, Jed! I just *hate* to see you ruining your life this way. Can't you see that you're wasting time with those— those playboys."

"Hey, whoa!" Jed said to stop her. Caitlin's sudden outburst was completely out of line as far as he was concerned. After all, he was entitled to have friends, wasn't he? And so what if he went out a few nights a week? What was the big deal? "Look, Caitlin, I honestly don't appreciate your calling my friends names. And they *are* my friends," he stressed.

"Some friends!" she replied icily. "They're destroying you. Can't you see that?"

"What I see is that you're so busy writing articles for that magazine and becoming the big career girl that you don't have a heck of a lot of time left over for me. And who knows what will happen now that you're Little Miss Cover Model."

"Jed, that's not fair," Caitlin snapped back, hurt by his accusations. "You're the one who wanted to show me off tonight. I would have much rather gone someplace where we could have been alone. In fact, I didn't even want to go out at all. I was tired after a long day at work, and I would just as soon have put on some jeans and a sweatshirt. We could have ordered in a pizza and watched a video." She shook her head again. "No, Jed, don't you dare accuse me of not wanting to spend time with you." The ice slid back into her voice. "One thing I can definitely say about this evening is that I was *not* spending my time with you! No, I was just there as a prize you wanted to show off, to brag about." She paused before adding, "And I'm not going to do it again!"

They rode the rest of the way to Caitlin's apartment in strained silence. Caitlin stared stonily out the window on her side. When they reached her building and the cab had drawn up to the curb, she turned to Jed and quietly said goodnight. Then she got out and walked to the door without a backward glance.

10

Both their argument the previous night and Jed's call earlier that morning were on Caitlin's mind as she entered the *National* building at five minutes to nine.

Jed had called her just as she was getting out of the shower. She had stood in her bedroom dripping onto the carpet, a big towel wrapped around her. Without actually coming out and saying he was sorry, Jed had apologized for his behavior the night before. The strain between them was lessened somewhat, but not completely as far as Caitlin was concerned.

Striding toward the bank of elevators at the rear of the lobby, she told herself that she had been totally in the right when she had lashed out at Jed for wasting his time with those jerks he was hanging around with. She wasn't about to back down, either—she loved him too much. And it was too awful to think about him throwing away the chance to get his degree from Columbia. And that was exactly what he'd be doing if he kept on acting the way he was! *If only there was something I could do*, Caitlin thought. *Maybe, if I talk to Melanie, she might have an idea of what*—"

"Hey, Caitlin!" Peter Leonard called, interrupting her thoughts. "Wait a second." Coming up beside her, he took her arm.

"Oh, Peter, hi!" She paused, confused by the urgent look on his face. "What is it? What's going on? Can we talk in the elevator—I've got to get upstairs."

"No, you don't." Peter turned her around so that they were now walking back toward the lobby door. "You're going across the street with me for a cup of coffee. And don't worry," he said as she started to protest, "Arlene knows all about it. In fact, she highly approves. I have her permission to keep you away from your desk for an hour, longer if that's what it takes."

"If that's what *what* takes?" Caitlin asked, laughing lightly at Peter's mysterious behavior. "Tell me now."

"No, not yet," Peter said, "Be patient. This is not something I want to try and explain while we're crossing Fifth Avenue at nine o'clock in the morning." With that, he pulled her with him as he dashed across the street.

A few minutes later they were sitting in one of the back booths of a nearby deli, and a waitress was setting down the coffee they had ordered.

"Okay, now that you've successfully kidnapped me," Caitlin said, "would you mind explaining what's going on?"

"All right, here goes," Peter said, eyes flashing with suppressed excitement. "Have you ever heard of Amalie Gray Cosmetics?"

"Of course I have," Caitlin replied, still looking confused. "I even use some of their products—Amalie Gray's facial soap is terrific."

"You use their stuff?" Peter repeated, leaning toward her. He shook his head. "This is just too perfect! They want you to represent their perfume, Misty Morn."

"Who does? *Amalie Gray*?" Caitlin was staring incredulously at Peter.

"You got it! The people at the ad agency that handles the Amalie Gray account saw you on the *National* cover. They think you'd be great as the Misty Morn girl. You know, like Revlon's Charlie girl. Well, anyway, they talked to the people at Amalie Gray and they agreed wholeheartedly. And, of course, I think they're absolutely right!" He grinned. "But the best part is that they want us to work together—I'd be your photographer for the ads." Something in Caitlin's expression made Peter pause. "You don't like the idea of my being your photographer?"

"No. I mean—uh—" Caitlin shook her head. "Peter, you're going too fast for me. Look, I can't tell you how flattered I am that they want to use me, but I don't want to do any modeling." Emphasizing her next words, she put her hands flat on the table. "I want to be a news writer— hopefully at *National*—and Arlene is just now starting to give me some assignments. But, because I'm also still her assistant, I have to do a lot of that writing at home in the evening." She took a deep breath. "Peter, I don't want to give up those assignments, and I don't see how I could do them *and* the modeling."

"But wait," he said, putting his hand over hers. "Just listen for a minute and let me explain, okay. You see, I have this friend over at Klein and Smith Advertising, and he was the one who thought of using you for the Amalie Gray account. He called me because he knew I took the photograph of you that was on the *National* cover. Anyway, I was sure that before you would agree to do this, you would consider your writing career. So, I asked my friend just how much time this assignment would take. Caitlin," he said, the enthusiasm building in his voice, "it won't take up much of your time. They could do most of the shoots in the morning before work, or on the weekends. All you'd be giving up would be an extra hour of sleep here and there. That's not much when you think of what this will mean—your photograph in every magazine, the glamour, the excitement, the *money*."

"I don't care about the money, Peter," she protested. Still, it *was* beginning to sound kind of exciting. Sighing, she shook her head. "Oh, Peter—"

"Caitlin," he interrupted, "this is the kind of opportunity most girls only dream of. Those ads are going to be featured in every major fashion magazine in the country. In only a few months the whole world will know you as the Misty Morn girl. Come on, Caitlin, say you'll do it."

"All right, all right," Caitlin finally agreed, unable to resist the pleading look on Peter's face. "You've convinced me. I'll do it. So, what do I have to do first?"

"Well, first you need to sign a contract," Peter answered with a light laugh at Caitlin's businesslike manner. "Someone from the agency will contact you later this afternoon. After that, we go to work."

Caitlin's first scheduled shoot with Peter was for ten days later. Supposedly that would be plenty of time, but there seemed to be hardly enough hours in the day to fit in everything that needed to be done. She had to go to meetings with the ad agency, with Amalie Gray herself, with the cosmetic firm's lawyers to sign the contracts, with the public relations or PR people to go over her background in order to set up publicity releases. There were fittings for the clothes she would be wearing in the photographs, test shots to check the colors of the costumes and the makeup, and a session with the hair stylist, who, in the end, gave in and agreed that her heavy silken mane of black hair was perfect as it was.

This was all in addition to having to complete the articles she was currently working on, as well as sitting down one afternoon with Arlene to go over the new articles she was assigning her.

Still, Caitlin managed to squeeze in some time to be with Jed. Unfortunately, when they did see each other, things did not go smoothly. Instead of being romantic, the times she spent with Jed were tense. Caitlin would sit with him over a glass of white wine and nod tiredly as he talked about his friends. Even when he did seem interested in what she was doing, she couldn't find the energy to explain everything. Still, she promised herself that all that would change once those initial meetings were finished.

The agency had gone along with Peter's initial

idea for the campaign, which was to shoot Caitlin at various locations around the city at sunrise in order to achieve an ethereal effect with the early-morning light. It was a perfect way to highlight the product—Misty Morn. And with Caitlin's fine classic, bone structure, the results were nothing less than sensational. In Peter's photographs, her timeless beauty was captured perfectly. As one ad executive said, "It's like a painting by one of those eighteenth century masters." Everyone was delighted—most of all Peter, who seemed to be falling more and more under Caitlin's spell.

They shot at several locations. One series was done in Central Park, with the mist rising off The Lake and Caitlin dressed in clouds of pale rose silk. Another one featured Caitlin seated on the back of one of the stone lions in front of the main branch of the public library.

"Straight from Narnia," Peter said, helping her down.

"And you have the right name to be my hero," Caitlin said with a teasing smile, referring to the character named Peter from *The Lion, the Witch, and the Wardrobe.*

"Of course," he said in a low voice, holding her briefly before letting her go.

On still another day they were at Lincoln Center. Peter had put a lone cellist wearing tails in the background, and Caitlin was in a satin evening dress. After the shoot was finished, Peter brought her a light coat and put it around her shoulders. As they walked over to the table that had been freshly stocked with coffee and doughnuts, Peter casually asked her if she would like to do a little private modeling for him.

"I'd like to do an entire series of you for the one-man show my agent is setting up for me in the spring. I'm not quite sure how I'd do it, but you photograph with such intensity. I think it could be an exceptional series."

"Well," Caitlin said tentatively as she took the cup of steaming coffee he handed her. "That sounds intriguing." She did like working with Peter. And she could imagine that some day his name would rank along with the great portrait photographers like Richard Avedon and Annie Liebowitz. "But, you know how I feel about my time," she said.

"It would only take a few shoots. And we could work at my studio, not the magazine studio. You could even call the shots as far as choosing the days you want to work. Just a couple of sessions. Tops."

Caitlin ended up agreeing to it as long as she could fit it into her Amalie Gray schedule and her work schedule. But when she told Jed, he wasn't happy at all.

"You're going to spend your evenings in his

studio? At his home? Alone?" Jed stared at her, then shook his head at what he obviously considered her complete naiveté. "Caitlin, how could you fall for a line that's that ancient?" He shook his head, scowling. "I mean, why didn't he just come right out and ask if you'd like to come up and see his etchings?"

"You're wrong about Peter, Jed," Caitlin argued. "If you knew Peter the way I do, you'd never even dream of saying something like that. He's an absolute professional. To him, I'm just like anything else he might photograph"—she searched for an example—"like a bowl of fruit or a vase of flowers."

"Ha!" Jed said. "Tell me, Caitlin, has anyone tried to sell you the Brooklyn Bridge lately?"

"Jed, you can stop that right now. You're plainly jealous, and you have absolutely no reason to be. Now let's change the subject."

Caitlin began modeling at Peter's studio soon after her horrible scene with Jed. And Peter was just as professional as she had told Jed he would be. But, as the weeks went by, Peter found himself feeling more and more attracted to Caitlin. It wasn't just her beauty, either. He was drawn to her as a person. What had started as innocent flirting on his part when they'd first begun to work on the Misty Morn ads had now turned serious for him.

And Jed, for his part, was certain that his suspicions about Peter were correct. He was so sure, in fact, that one morning he decided to see for himself exactly what Peter Leonard was like when he was with Caitlin. Without a word to her, he borrowed Chip's car and drove up to the location where they were doing an early-morning shoot. It was at the Cloisters, a graceful reconstruction of a medieval European monastery that had been assembled from pieces of many old monasteries. It had been constructed in a wooded park at the northern tip of Manhattan.

Peter had set up the shoot on a colonnaded walkway that ran along one side of an open courtyard. With the early morning sun slanting in across the top of the opposite wall, the walk's pale lavender shadows were broken up by bars of pale gold light. It was a very romantic setting.

Caitlin looked stunning in an ankle-length linen skirt and a deep purple camp shirt, standing as though she had just stepped out of the shadows. She carried a large, straw picture hat, into the brim of which had been stuck a small bunch of real violets.

For a long moment, as Jed stood hidden from view behind one of the weathered columns, he found himself completely caught up in the fantasy of the shot. While his hands were deep in the pockets of his wool-lined windbreaker, the collar turned up against the early morning chill, he was almost positive that fifty feet away from him where Caitlin stood, it was early summer instead of early November.

Then the spell was broken. Peter, dressed in a warm parka and turtleneck sweater, walked into the scene to adjust the collar on Caitlin's shirt. Jed watched while Peter pushed a strand of hair gently away from Caitlin's face. It was so obvious to him that Peter was falling in love with Caitlin that Jed could barely keep from leaping from his hiding place, charging over to where Peter stood, and giving him a few choice words.

Yet he stayed where he was, his teeth clenched, until the session started wrapping up. Then he stepped out of the shadows to greet Caitlin with a forced smile. "Hi," he said, completely ignoring Peter. "I thought I'd surprise you and come up here so I could take you to breakfast." Raising his voice slightly, he pulled off his jacket meaning to drape it around her shoulders. "Doesn't *anyone* care that you're practically freezing to death?"

"Of course someone does," Peter answered. Carrying Caitlin's blue cashmere jacket, he put it around Caitlin's shoulders before Jed reached her. "She's our star." With a cold smile at Jed, he introduced himself. "Hello, there. I'm Peter Leonard. You must be Jed."

"How did you guess?" Jed snapped.

Before Peter could answer, however, Caitlin quickly moved to stand between them. Gently putting a hand on Jed's shoulder, she said, "This is a nice surprise, but I really don't understand what you're doing here. It is pretty early, for anyone."

"I—I just thought I'd take you to breakfast." He smiled at her. "Just a spur of the moment sort of thing."

"Oh." She smiled. "Well, that's terrific. I'll just be a second. I have to change." She motioned at her clothes. "I'll be with you in a minute."

As they drove back downtown in the car Jed had borrowed, Caitlin was quiet. She finally asked in a searching voice, "Jed? This is Thursday, don't you have a class this morning?"

"Uh, yeah." It was a class he hadn't been to in more than two weeks. "But I thought I'd skip it today." He flashed her an uneven smile. "Breakfast with you sounded much better."

"Oh." The smile she gave him didn't quite reach her eyes. "Thank you, Jed. That was sweet." She studied the traffic for a moment, then turned to him again. "Jed, why did you *really* come to the shoot? Was it to see what Peter was like?"

"No!" he answered a little too quickly. "Of course not."

"It was, wasn't it?" She countered in a soft, disappointed tone. "Jed, I don't want to go to breakfast anymore. Just take me home."

"Caitlin, please," he said, forcing himself to keep his eyes on the road. "You don't have to eat anything if you don't want to. We can just talk." Spotting a coffee shop halfway down the block, he pulled into the first parking space he saw. He shut off the motor and turned to look at Caitlin. "How about a cup of coffee?"

"Jed, it's just that I'm so disappointed in you. Don't you see what this means?" She shook her head. "It means you don't trust me. I told you there was nothing going on between Peter and me, but you had to come see for yourself."

"All right, all right. I'll admit it. That's exactly what I did." He put his hand on the back of the seat and gripped the edge. "But, Caitlin, what I saw proved to me that I was right. That guy's crazy about you. It's so obvious that even a five-year-old could see it. I don't understand why you can't."

The anguish in Jed's voice made Caitlin look closer at him, and she realized that he really was concerned. "Jed—Jed, listen to me," she said, her voice now soft. "You are being ridiculous. I promise you, Peter has never acted toward me in any way other than the way a photographer would act with a model."

"He's in love with you," Jed insisted.

"He is not." She reached up and gently brushed her hand against the side of his face. "And even if he were, it wouldn't make the slightest bit of difference." She stared into his green eyes. "Because you, Jed Michaels, are the only man I will ever love."

"Oh, Caitlin, is that a promise?"

"Yes, Jed, that's a promise." She looked at him with love in her eyes.

He leaned over and kissed her gently, tenderly.

"Now," she said in a warm, breathy voice as she pulled away. "If you hurry and drop me off at my apartment, maybe you can still make that class."

11

Two days later Caitlin was in her apartment talking to Morgan, who had just stopped by to return a blouse she'd borrowed. Both girls were sitting on the couch, and Caitlin was telling Morgan about something that had happened that day.

"Laurence? Laurence Baxter?" Morgan's eyes widened in surprise. "Our Laurence from Highgate came up here from Virginia to interview you? How wild! I didn't even know he was a reporter on a newspaper."

"Yes," Caitlin replied, nodding. "And as far as I could tell, he's very good one, too. We did the interview this afternoon." She shrugged modestly. "It was a hoot—you know, local girl makes good and all that."

"Hey, that's great," Morgan said. Then a

faraway look came over her face. "You know, it seems funny to think about Laurence being a reporter. I mean, he was always so reserved. I can't imagine him asking perfect strangers probing questions about their lives." She glanced at Caitlin. "Anyway, I thought he wanted to go into computers."

"I think the shyness wore off when he was at Harvard," Caitlin replied. "When I talked to him, he said he became interested in being a reporter after he got involved in writing for the Harvard paper, the *Crimson*," she said with a smile. "He was really very self-assured this afternoon."

"Is he still as good-looking as he was when we were at Highgate together? He was always such a cutie."

"He definitely is, but in a slightly more mature way."

"Oh, really?" Morgan gave Caitlin a sly look. "Does that mean that Jed might have something to worry about? As I recall," she said teasingly, "you and Laurence did date during our junior year."

"Don't be so suspicious," she said back lightly. "Jed has positively nothing to be concerned about. Anything Laurence and I might have felt for each other is in the past. I consider him a good friend, but that's it."

"Oh, all right," Morgan said, giving a dismissive shrug. "So, is he on his way back to Virginia?"

"No, he's not leaving until first thing Monday morning. In fact, I invited him to have dinner with Jed and me tonight for my birthday. And, I've invited Melanie, too. It'll be kind of like a double date. Jed made reservations at Patsy's, that great Italian place over on Fifty-sixth Street. I asked to go there because they've got great pasta, and the atmosphere's so friendly. I thought we could just sit around and talk about old times." Silently she added herself that they were also less likely to encounter any of Jed's new friends there.

"Sounds nice, but what about Melanie?" Morgan wanted to know. "She doesn't even know Laurence, does she? I mean, what is she going to do while you and Jed and Laurence are reliving your years at Highgate? Isn't she going to feel slightly left out?"

"Come on, Morgan," Caitlin said. "You know I would never be so rude as to keep the conversation on one subject. There's sure to be something that Melanie and Laurence will share an interest in." Her eyes twinkled. "Besides, I think Melanie will enjoy being paired with someone as handsome and sophisticated as Laurence."

"I'm sure." Suddenly Morgan appeared thoughtful, and she stared into her lap for a moment before looking back up. Her face was now serious. "Speaking of Jed's sister, I've been meaning to tell you something, but I didn't know if I should. I mean, it's really none of my business, but if she were my sister—"

"Morgan, what is it?" Caitlin cut in, her voice concerned.

"Okay." Morgan nodded. She paused for a moment, trying to decide how to start. "You know that I go to a lot of parties and stuff for my gossip column. Right?" Caitlin nodded. "Well, in the last month I've been to a couple of parties down in the Village, that were—uh—kind of well—you know, every kind of booze there is, drugs in the bathroom, that sort of thing."

"Melanie was there?" Caitlin broke in, horrified.

"Uh-huh." Morgan nodded. "I've seen her twice, and both times she was with the same guy. Caitlin, he's a real loser. The word around is that he doesn't treat his girlfriends that well, either. Melanie might be in over her head."

"Thanks for telling me, Morgan," Caitlin said with real concern. "I like Melanie a lot, and I hate hearing that she's doing that sort of thing. Oh, why would she run around with that kind of group."

"What are you going to do? Are you going to tell Jed?" Morgan asked.

"No," Caitlin replied after thinking for a

moment. "I think I'll try to talk to her myself. We get along pretty well. But not until after tonight. Who knows," she smiled weakly, "maybe she'll forget all about that creep in the Village once she meets Laurence."

The dinner *had* gone well, Caitlin thought the next morning as she hung up the phone. The call had been from Laurence, who had wanted to thank her for everything she'd done for him during his brief stay.

Pouring a cup of coffee, Caitlin leaned against the kitchen counter for a moment and went over the events of the evening before.

The food had been excellent, and everyone had really seemed to enjoy themselves. Especially Jed. While he and Laurence had talked about their days at Highgate, Jed had been more like himself than in months. It seemed to Caitlin as though talking about a time before his father's death had made the tragedy disappear for a while. Jed was like a kid again.

And Melanie had looked marvelous. She and Laurence had sat together, and Caitlin remembered thinking they made a nice-looking couple. Melanie had worn a pale pink angora sweater over winter white wool slacks. Her light brown curls had been cut short since the last time Caitlin had seen her, and, Caitlin decided, the style was soft and flattering. She wore no makeup except some pink lipstick, and Caitlin had a difficult time thinking that this was the same girl Morgan had seen at those wild parties in the Village. Furthermore, the way Melanie had hung on every word Laurence had said had made her seem rather innocent.

Caitlin smiled to herself and sipped her coffee. Perhaps Melanie had more common sense than she'd given her credit for. Especially considering one of Laurence's last comments on the phone just then—that he'd asked Melanie if she'd have dinner with him the next time he was in New York. Melanie, of course, had said yes. "So," he told Caitlin, "it looks as though we might be seeing one another again soon. I really like Melanie, and I don't plan on this first date being our last."

Caitlin smiled to herself as she went into her bedroom and began to get ready for work. Maybe everything would work out after all. Melanie and Laurence had certainly gotten along, and he could only be a good influence on her. And Jed had seemed like his old self again. She looked over at the lovely, limited-edition print he had bought her for her birthday, thinking for the millionth time how beautiful it was. Jed had certainly outdone himself this time.

* * *

As winter was approaching, the days were shorter, and that meant that the morning light was changing. Peter, feeling the need to hurry and complete the final Misty Morn shots, moved up the shooting schedule. This put an even greater demand on Caitlin's energy as well as her time. But she kept right on trying to do everything, including seeing Jed.

During that week after her birthday, she was finding it more and more difficult to continue to juggle the separate photo sessions, her work at *National*, and seeing Jed on the weekends. She was walking around in a state of physical exhaustion and becoming more and more dissatisfied with modeling. And it was made even worse by the fact that she suspected Jed was running around with his friends more and more because he was never at home in the evenings.

But Caitlin kept on telling herself the photo sessions would end soon, and then she would be able to see Jed more often.

Melanie, though, was another matter. On Tuesday, a week and half after her birthday, as Caitlin was coming back from work, she ran into Morgan in the lobby of their building.

"I hate to be the bearer of bad news," Morgan said after they'd exchanged hellos. "But I saw Melanie at another one of those parties. And she looked really wasted."

"Melanie was drunk?" Caitlin gasped.

"I'm pretty sure," Morgan said. "It was a pretty rough crowd, and I didn't want to stay. I told my date to take me home, or else I would grab a cab and go home alone." She smiled grimly. "Good thing I had enough money for a cab."

"Oh, that's too bad." Caitlin sympathized distractedly. But she was less concerned about Morgan's unfortunate taste in dates than she was with Melanie. "Look, thanks for telling me, Morgan," she said. "This time, I'm definitely going to talk to Melanie and see what I can do." She glanced at her watch. "In fact, I think I'll run over to their apartment right now and see if I can catch her in."

Melanie was there, and Caitlin came right to the point. After that, Melanie wasn't interested in having her stay any longer.

"Look," she said, facing Caitlin across the spacious living room, "I'm a big girl, and I can live my own life now. I don't need you or my brother telling me what to do."

As Caitlin listened to Melanie, she remembered the last time that she had looked at her surrounded by this same furniture: it was back in Montana, just after Melanie had discovered that their father had left the ranch to their mother. *Poor Melanie*, she thought. It was bad enough that she had just lost her father, but to be estranged from her mother at such a trying time must be doubly hard. No wonder she was having trouble finding a direction in her life. But just as Caitlin began to soften toward Jed's sister, Melanie started hurling angry words again.

"And if you're thinking about telling Jed," she spat out, "you might as well forget it. He's too busy having his own fun to be concerned about me."

"But what about school, Melanie?" Caitlin countered. "You can't party the way you are now, and still keep up in your classes."

"Oh, have I got news for you, Caitlin!" Melanie said in a flat voice. "I've already dropped out of NYU—two weeks ago." She gave a bored shrug. "That's a dull place to spend your time." "And don't ask me what I plan to do with my time, because I'll just tell you that it's none of your damned business. Got that?" Not waiting for a reply, she turned and stormed off toward her bedroom at the other side of the room. There she turned to face Caitlin again. "You can let yourself out whenever you get tired of being in my living room by yourself," she said. Then she went into her room and slammed the door shut.

After listening to Melanie's outburst, Caitlin's first thought was to talk to Jed. So back in her own apartment two hours later she did call him and tell him about her conversation with Melanie.

"Jed, I'm really worried about her," Caitlin said. "From what Morgan told me, she's getting in way over her head. The kind of people who go to those parties play pretty rough, you know."

"I think you're overreacting, Caitlin," Jed replied. "You know what a gossip Morgan is. She's probably just trying to stir things up a little."

"But—" Caitlin began.

"Look, don't worry about Melanie," Jed said in a smooth voice. "She's smarter than you think."

Caitlin was furious at Jed's assured tone. He obviously wasn't going to listen to her no matter what she said.

A few minutes later, after hearing another of Jed's assurances that Melanie could take care of herself, Caitlin hung up. How much of his confidence in his younger sister, she wondered, was prompted by his own careless life-style? How could he see what a dangerous group she was getting involved with when he was hanging out with the same kind of people? Caitlin slumped down on the couch and sighed in frustration. What else could she do?

12

Swallowing her disappointment in Jed, Caitlin went to work the next morning determined to make it a good day. There were several projects she had had to put on hold during the last two weeks of her heavier shooting schedule, and she was determined to finish them up by the end of the day.

When she got to work, however, she found Peter waiting at her cubicle, eager to tell her something. The minute she walked in and saw the telltale excitement in his eyes, she had a sinking feeling she was not going to get those projects finished after all.

Before she could even say "good morning," he was already launching into his news. He told her that the people at Amalie Gray wanted her to do another shoot. "It would just be a single location—the lovely, tropical island of Saint Martin. The shoot is this weekend, Caitlin, but it's just for two days. Think of it as a vacation—the sun, the palm trees, clear blue waters, the best hotel accommodations." With a shrug, he spread his hands. "Then you'll be right back here in New York, in the middle of this dismal rain we've been having." He paused to let the last bit sink in. "So what do you say?"

Caitlin sighed. "I don't know, Peter. Right now I don't even want to have to think about facing another camera." She cast him a pleading look. "Can't they get someone else?"

"No way!" he said emphatically. "They want you and only you, Caitlin. The ad we'd be shooting is for their new Misty Morn fragrance, and they've really built their campaign around you." He smiled. "Besides, they really love working with you."

"Would I be violating my contract if I refused to go?"

"Well—no," Peter said, obviously not happy over how she was acting. "Your contract only covers the original Misty Morn fragrance."

"Peter—" It made her feel guilty for not being as excited about the trip as he obviously was. But she really didn't want to go. "Give me until tomorrow to think about an answer, okay?"

Peter left, looking morose. Moments later Caitlin's phone rang. It was Arlene, asking her to come into her office. "I've got an assignment I think you're really going to like," she promised in a cheerful voice.

The assignment turned out to be a chance to do an interview with Brent Lowe, a hot, new television star. He was on a publicity tour and would only be in New York for one day. "The interview should be good for both of your careers, and hopefully it will sell a few magazines, too," Arlene explained. "Six months ago, no one had heard of either of you. Now, you're both generating a lot of interest. And you're both about the same age. He's not too hard on the eyes, either," she added with a laugh. "If I were five years younger, I'd do the interview myself. So, if you can clear your calendar for Saturday afternoon, I'll—"

"Saturday?" Caitlin asked, slumping back in her chair. If she agreed to go on location with Peter, she would be posing on a beach in the middle of the Caribbean on Saturday. How could this be happening to her? A plum assignment like an interview with Brent Lowe didn't come along every day.

"Caitlin?" Arlene asked, leaning toward her. "Is there a problem?"

"Arlene," Caitlin said in a dejected tone. "I'm afraid I might have a schedule conflict." Then she went on to explain about Peter and the shoot.

127

"Hmmm." Arlene nodded and frowned when Caitlin finished. "Well, I can always get someone else to do the interview. That's certainly no problem. It's just that I'd rather see you do it. It could really be a boost for you in terms of getting you bigger assignments later on." She shook her head. "No, it wasn't fair of me to try to pressure you like that. I understand the chance to do that shoot for Amalie Gray is important." Smiling kindly at Caitlin, she said, "I'll tell you what, I'll hold off giving the assignment to anyone else until tomorrow morning to give you time to think. But I'll have to have a firm decision by then—at say nine o'clock?"

"Thank you, Arlene. I appreciate it," Caitlin replied, standing. "I'll talk to you later." She left, hating the decision she had to make.

She continued to wrestle with the pros and cons of both offers for the rest of the morning. Finally, at noon, she felt she simply had to get away from the office, even though it had been pouring rain all morning. Everyone else was ordering lunch from the deli across the street.

An hour later she returned, having had a walk and gone to a nearby restaurant where she toyed with a club sandwich for twenty minutes before finally admitting to herself that she wasn't hungry. Walking down the aisle toward her cubicle, she passed two secretaries who gave her secretive smiles that she didn't understand until she spotted the florist's vase of yellow roses sitting on the corner of her desk. "Now who—" she said, reaching for the small envelope. Slipping the card out, she read the short message, "Forgive me? Jed."

Holding the card, she suddenly felt a lot better. With a tender smile, she reached out to touch the petals on one of the partially opened flowers. But the phone rang before her finger met with the velvet surface. She picked up the receiver. "Yes," she said softly, before remembering she was talking on a business phone. Clearing her throat, she said, "Hello, this is Caitlin Ryan."

"And this is Jed Michaels," Jed's low, warm voice came over the line. "Uh—do I dare assume from your first answer that you've gotten the roses, and that you still love me?" She was about to reply, but he went right on. "I hope so because I'd like you to accept my invitation to my apartment to dinner tonight. I'd like to make a proper apology for the lousy way I've been acting lately. I know now that I should have been a lot more understanding while you were working all those long hours." He paused. "So, am I forgiven?"

"Well—" Caitlin said, teasing him happily. "Let me see. I guess I could give some thought to accepting your invitation. Tell me, Jed, in case I decide to come, what time would dinner be?"

"About eight?"

"Sounds great." Caitlin laughed, feeling for the first time in days that the world was all right again. "I'll be there, and I'll bring the wine."

Jed broiled thick steaks for dinner, serving them with baked potatoes and an endive salad. Caitlin had gone home after work and changed into comfortable wool slacks and a bulky turquoise sweater before taking a cab to Jed's. On the way she stopped to pick up a bottle of Pinot Noir as she had promised she would.

By the time Caitlin got there, Melanie had already left to go out for the evening. And without either of them having to say a word, it was silently agreed that she would not be a topic of discussion during dinner or afterward. Cutting into her beautifully done steak, Caitlin told herself that she would stick to neutral subjects. All she wanted was for her relationship with Jed to go back to being as wonderful as it had once been. She hoped that that night would help her accomplish that.

Once the dishes were cleared away, Jed put a match to the fire that was already laid in the fireplace, then he put a tape of soft music on the stereo. Caitlin, meanwhile, carried the half-finished bottle of wine and their glasses over to the coffee table in front of the couch. After lowering the lights, Jed crossed over to sit beside her, putting his arm around her shoulders so she could lean against his chest.

The rain was still coming down outside, and it made a soothing counterpoint to the taped music. Caitlin smiled contentedly as she sipped her wine. The evening truly was turning out to be wonderful. She couldn't imagine wanting to be anywhere but there—with Jed. She was so happy being there that she felt as if she were in a cocoon.

She felt protected and safe, curled up beside him. Staring thoughtfully into the dancing fire, she wondered if she should risk upsetting Jed by asking him his advice about the decision she still had to make before morning. But then, she decided, why ruin a marvelous evening if there was a possibility she might be bringing up something to do with Peter. Yet, she trusted Jed, and she really wanted his input.

Jed finally made up her mind for her. "What's the matter, Caitlin? You've been deep in thought for the past five minutes. I can always tell by that little worry line you get." Lifting a finger, he gently traced it across her forehead. "Right there. You know, if you've got a problem, I want to share it. Maybe I can even help you sort it out."

"Oh, Jed," she said relieved. "I'm so glad you feel that way." She pulled away from him and sat up just enough so that she could look into his face as she talked. "I've been wrestling with a huge decision all day."

Caitlin then told him about the choice she had to make between staying in New York and doing the interview and going off to Saint Martin with Peter to do the shoot. Jed's face was partially hidden in the shadows, and Caitlin didn't notice the scowl that began to develop on it as she began talking about Peter. It deepened as she went on. She had been just about to say that she really thought she wanted to stay in New York and do the interview when Jed suddenly interrupted her.

"I don't believe it!" he cried out. And with an angry motion, he yanked his hand away from around her shoulder. Staring at her, he said, "You're asking me if you should go off to some secluded island with Lover-Boy Leonard?" He ran his hand through his hair. "Oh, I don't believe it! I just don't believe it!"

"Jed!" Caitlin was sitting straight up at the edge of the couch. "I don't believe *you*." She shook her head in amazement. "I'm hardly talking about a romantic weekend. This would be strictly a business trip—to shoot some photographs for an ad campaign. Surely by now you've seen how much hard work that is. And other people would be with us, romance is the last thing anyone thinks about during a shoot.

Or after one for that matter. And even so, I've told you a million times—"

"I'll bet Peter wouldn't be too tired," Jed yelled. Leaping up, he stalked over to the fireplace, jammed his hands into his pockets, and rocked on his heels as he stared at the leaping flames. Caitlin could see the muscle along his jaw twitching. Then he turned around, jabbing a finger in her direction. "You're not going!"

"What do you mean I'm not going?" she cried. "Are you saying that you're *forbidding* me to go?"

"That's exactly what I'm doing," Jed shot back. "I've told you before that Peter Leonard is after you. It's bad enough that I have to think about you posing for him here, in New York. But thousands of miles away on some island?"

"At a crowded resort, with a stylist and makeup person," she interrupted in exasperation.

"I can see it now," he went on. "The warm night, dancing beneath a tropical moon, a couple of those rum drinks—"

"That does it!" Furious, Caitlin got to her feet, her eyes blazing. "I know what you've told me, but I also know what I've told you. Peter is always strictly business, and there is nothing between us but friendship and respect. But, if you wish to think otherwise, I can't stop you. I am, however, not about to stick around to watch you stew in your suspicions." Walking quickly to the chair where she'd left her coat and purse, she snatched them up. She shoved her arms into the sleeves, and yanked the collar into place. "I'm leaving." She paused to look directly at him. "And the day after tomorrow, I'm leaving for Saint Martin."

"Caitlin, wait!" Jed yelled.

But Caitlin was out of the door and on her way down the hall. Jed came after her, but she ran down the six flights of stairs and out the front door too quickly for him to catch her. She was so angry she could barely think straight. Yet, one thing stood out clearly in her mind. Jed, forbidding her to go with Peter, had forced her into saying she would go. She had to go now, to prove that she was her own person.

13

Exhausted, Caitlin unlocked the door to her private bungalow and went inside. Barely noticing the fresh fruit basket that had been delivered in her absence, she went into the bedroom. There she kicked off her sandals, dropped her bulky totebag on the floor, and flopped onto the soft cushions of a rattan chaise longue. Lifting her hair away from her neck, she lay back and closed her eyes, letting the gentle hum of the air conditioner soothe her tired mind.

She was still wearing the bathing suit and matching cover from the last setup of the day. There had been several different summer outfits, and she was allowed to keep all of them. Definitely a nice bonus, she thought, considering they were the newest designs.

The shoot had gone well but it had been a long

day. Caitlin had been up since four-thirty that morning. She had had to crawl from bed that early in order to shower and wash her hair and be ready for the first early-morning shot.

They had flown into Saint Martin from New York late the previous afternoon. From the moment the plane had landed, coming in low over a bay that was dyed molten gold by a setting sun, Caitlin had fallen under the spell of the island's tropical beauty. "Oh, Peter," she had exclaimed, "this is heaven! I have always loved the Caribbean. I think I might have to stay for a week instead of only two days. No, on second thought, make that a month. A month here would be just about right."

Peter had laughed, delighted to see Caitlin happy. The gloomy expression she had worn to the airport in New York had finally vanished. "What did I tell you? And just wait until you see the hotel. You'll want to stay for a year!"

The hotel was as beautiful as Peter had promised it would be. It had once been a private estate, with the central building surrounded by about twenty private bungalows. The bungalows were shaded by tall palms and bougainvillea blossoms cascaded over nearly every wall.

The bungalow Caitlin was given came complete with a living room, a bedroom and separate dressing room, plus a tiny kitchen. The refrigerator was stocked with soft drinks, club soda, mineral water, and a selection of cheeses and chocolates as well. "And, of course you may order whatever else you might want from room service," the bellman had said as he set her luggage down.

Walking over to the white drapes that ran the length of one side of the living room, the bellman opened them to reveal a private pool. The pool had been made to look as though it were part of the natural landscape, with rocks that jutted out over the surface of the water and a splashing waterfall.

"How gorgeous," Caitlin gasped. Her comment seemed to please the bellman almost as much as the generous tip she gave him.

As soon as he left, she changed into one of her own bathing suits and went for a swim. Then, refreshed, she had slipped into a loose-fitting jumpsuit, unpacked her clothes, and called Peter to see what time he wanted her ready the next morning. Next she called room service and ordered a dinner of cold shrimp and fresh fruit. As soon as she finished eating it, she fell asleep, lulled by the sounds of the night birds and the pool waterfall.

Now, as she lay there, exhausted from her day's work, she wished she could again take a quick swim and then order something from room service. But that was out of the question. Peter, delighted by the way the shoot had gone, insisted that they celebrate by having dinner in the hotel's dining room. "You'll love it, Caitlin," he told her. "Actually it's not a room at all. It's an open courtyard with only the stars overhead. The food is excellent, too. At least it was the last time I was here. In case you feel like dancing after dinner, there's even a small orchestra."

Caitlin sighed. She was going to have to get up, shower, and do her hair and her makeup again. Well, she thought, opening her eyes and stretching, at least she'd brought something to wear.

As Caitlin walked toward Peter, who was waiting for her at the entrance to the dining room, he was amazed again by her beauty. He'd never known anyone like her. Two hours earlier she had been a sea nymph, emerging from the surf to tease and flirt with his camera. Now she was cool and sophisticated, dressed in a pale blue silk dress, her hair swept to the side so that it lay in a shining wave against her slender neck. And he couldn't help but notice, as the maître'd showed them through the restaurant to their table, that nearly every man there gave Caitlin an admiring glance.

We do make a handsome couple, Peter thought as he helped her into her chair. Then he went around to his own seat, smoothing a hand automatically down the front of his dinner jacket as he sat down. The maître'd then handed them menus. "Your waiter will be with you shortly."

"So what do you think?" Peter asked after a moment.

"I think it's really beautiful," Caitlin replied.

She looked around. Their table was placed far enough apart from the others to assure a feeling of privacy. It was set with a heavy white cloth, glistening silver and crystal, and a centerpiece of one white candle inside a glass chimney—to keep the soft breeze from blowing out the flame. Graceful ferns and earthen pots of fragrant flowers were placed in clusters on the tile floor, and in the trees surrounding the courtyard, tiny white lights blinked, mirroring the stars overhead. And a small string orchestra played on a raised dais next to a small dance floor.

"It's even more than you promised," she said. Laying down her menu, she smiled. "I think I'll take your word for the food as well. Why don't you order for me."

When the waiter came over, Peter ordered the blackened chicken, which was served with wild rice and slices of fresh mango, dressed with lime. With an agreeing nod, the waiter picked up the menus and left.

Peter grinned at her. "I have a feeling you're wondering if you were right to leave the decision to me," he said with a small laugh. "But trust me, blackened chicken doesn't mean that it will be burned. You see, it's prepared by first roasting a heavy layer of hot spices in the bottom of a pan. Then the chicken is placed on top of that until it's so tender it practically falls apart. It's pretty spicy, but the fruit helps when you've gotten a mouthful that's too hot."

"Ummm. Sounds good," Caitlin said, her eyes shining. "I like trying different foods."

"Ah, a girl after my own heart," he said. Then he thought how true that really was. Looking at her sitting across from him, he was positive that he loved her. And she seemed to care for him, too. He knew that she'd given up an important interview to come to Saint Martin. That meant something. And he was sure that her relationship with Jed Michaels was on the rocks. From what Caitlin told him, Jed had been acting like a jerk. He didn't deserve her. No, Caitlin should have a man who wasn't wrapped up in his own problems—someone like himself. Someone who would—

Peter's thoughts were interrupted by the owner of the hotel who had come over to their table. He was a graying, older gentleman with sparkling dark eyes. A waiter followed closely behind him, carrying a bottle of iced champagne and two champagne flutes.

"Ah Mademoiselle Ryan, Monsieur Lenoard," he said. "I hope you will allow me to offer you this fine bottle of champagne." With a dramatic gesture, he motioned for the waiter to put down the glasses and to open the bottle. "I watched you as you worked together today, and I said to myself, 'Rollo, these two are truly in love, no?'" The waiter carefully twisted the cork so that it only made a tiny popping sound as it came out. Then he began to pour. Beaming, the owner looked down at Peter. "You are a very lucky man to have such a lovely lady. Enjoy the champagne."

Because Peter seemed to be at a momentary loss for words, Caitlin spoke. "Thank you," she said with a thoughtful smile. "That was lovely of you." She watched as he backed away, gave a little half bow, then turned and motioned for the waiter to follow him again. She looked back at Peter and laughed with delight. "Oh, Peter, wasn't that sweet of him?" Shaking her head, she added, "But how could he be so wrong about us? Can you picture us being a couple?" She started to laugh again, but then, looking at Peter's expression, the laughter died in her throat. Something was wrong. He looked stunned. No, perhaps that was too strong a word. It was more as if someone had just given him some bad news. "Peter?" She leaned in toward him, asking quietly, "Are you all right? Are you feeling okay? It has been a long day, and we were out in the sun for most of it." She reached across the table to touch his cheek.

"No! Don't," he said, pulling back. Then, apologetically he shook his head. "I'm sorry. I didn't mean to react that way. It's just that—" He stopped speaking and looked away from her, a frown furrowing his brow. After a long moment he looked back at her. "Caitlin, part of what Rollo said just now is true." His mouth twisted in a wry smile. "When he looked at me, he *did* see a person in love. You see, Caitlin, I do love you." He saw the surprise on Caitlin's face and hurried on. "Frankly, I'd begun to think you might feel the same way. Especially when you gave up the opportunity to do that interview this weekend to come down here with me."

"Oh, Peter . . ." Caitlin's voice trailed off as she realized how she must have hurt him by laughing at what the owner had said. But how could he have taken her decision to come to Saint Martin as a signal that she was in love with him? It was just business, he should know that. "Peter, I like you very much. And I admire you. You're one of the most interesting and talented people I've ever met. But—"

"But you don't love me," he added harshly.

"Peter, I don't know what else to say." Feeling helpless, she shrugged and dropped her hands into her lap.

"Oh, I think you've said it all." His gaze dropped from her face to the candle on the table between them. Then he looked back up at her. "We certainly shouldn't waste the finest champagne the house has to offer—even if it is only for lovers." Picking up his glass, he downed it, then grabbed the bottle and poured himself another. He drank more than half of that before putting the glass back on the table. "There!" he said. "End of discussion." He glanced around, and in a strong voice that pained Caitlin, he said, "I wonder where our dinner is?"

It took a long time for Caitlin to fall asleep that night. For almost an hour before she finally crawled into bed, she stood leaning against the side of the open patio door, staring out at the lighted pool and at the stars.

Poor Peter. She felt so awful. But she also knew she had handled the situation the only way she could—by being straight forward about her own feelings.

She shook her head. *Jed was right all along.* Now she understood why he'd been acting the way he had. If she'd only listened to him, if they'd been able to sit down and talk, everything would have been straightened out by now. She wouldn't be in Saint Martin, she would be back in New York, with Jed, where she belonged.

Well, she reminded herself, she'd be flying home in the morning. Then she and Jed would have that talk, and then everything *would* be all right again. A happy smile on her lips, Caitlin finally fell asleep.

14

After Caitlin had stormed from the apartment Wednesday evening, Jed stood staring at the burning logs in the fireplace while his anger grew. Finally, in a sudden fury, he had picked up his wine glass and hurled it at the fire. The crystal had shattered, sending shards flying out across the brick and into the deep piled carpet. Jed had then grabbed his jacket and run out into the rainy night.

Jed's anger at Caitlin's refusal to believe him continued to grow. By Saturday he was prowling around his apartment, moving restlessly from room to room, obsessed with thinking about Caitlin down in the Caribbean with Peter Leonard.

"Damn him!" he muttered out loud. Pausing in front of the picture window in the living room, he stared out at the lights from New Jersey reflecting off the surface of the river. Frustrated, he ran his hand through his hair. Why couldn't Caitlin see what was going on? How could she be so blind? Peter's love for her was so obvious.

He glanced at his watch and shook his head. It was almost eight o'clock on a Saturday night, and there he was all alone. Melanie had gone off to a party. His friends were probably all out having dinner somewhere. What was Caitlin doing just then, he wondered. Going to dinner? Yeah, she would be out at dinner with Peter. Jed could picture the two of them—Caitlin in some silky dress, and Peter, looking sophisticated in a white dinner jacket. What would they do later? Dance? Yes, Peter would take Caitlin in his arms and— Making a fist, Jed slammed it against the wall.

He was so intent on his vision of Caitlin and Peter that a long time passed before he felt the pain. Then, glancing down at his hand, he felt the pain and saw the reddened area that would be a dark bruise in the morning. Self-pity welled up inside him. It was all Caitlin's fault! It was her fault that he'd hurt his hand. Well, he was not about to stay there and make himself even more miserable by thinking about her with Peter together on that tropical island.

Going quickly over to the desk, he began

searching through a pile of papers he had left by the phone. He remembered that someone had invited him to a party, one of those once-a-year bashes. A party like that was exactly what he needed. Lots of noise and lots of people to make him forget.

Two hours later, Jed climbed out of the cab that had pulled up to the curb outside the brownstone in the Village. He could hear the beat of the rock music that was coming through the closed front door. As the cab pulled away, Jed climbed the stairs and rang the bell. Moments later the front door opened and the sound of people laughing and talking washed over him.

The lavishly decorated townhouse was packed with young people. They were dressed in everything from jeans and sweatshirts to tuxes and silk dresses. Before he'd gotten five feet into the foyer a beer was pressed into his hand. He glanced at it, then raised it to his lips and took a large swallow. He didn't particularly like beer, but a drink was a drink. Moving toward the living room, he stopped when he heard a familiar voice purr close behind him. "Well, hello there, Jed. Imagine seeing you here."

Turning around, Jed found himself standing about two feet from a tall, beautiful blonde, dressed in an outrageous green-sequined top and tight black pants. "Nonnie!" he cried with a genuine smile. "Hello, yourself. It's good to see you." His gaze moved appreciatively over her. The beer was starting to relax him. "I seem to remember that you were wearing green the last time I saw you—at that party on the *Merry Gull*."

"Do I gather, then, that you like green?" Nonnie asked in a sexy voice, running a finger lightly down the lapel of his jacket. "Because if you do, I'll certainly wear it more often." And she would, she told herself, if she was going to get that kind of reaction. She had been after Jed Michaels since the first time she had seen him. But he had never seemed interested. But that night was different, very different. She could spot a guy who was out to forget someone, and she wasn't above helping the process along. She smiled.

"Hey, that's some smile," Jed said. "And, yes, I like the way you wear green.'

"Hello, hello, you two!" Chip cried, bursting toward them from the far side of the room. "Glad to see you, Jed. And, Nonnie, you look great with a capital G."

"Hey, wait just a minute!" A pretty redhead had followed Chip and now she put a hand on his shoulder. "Are you forgetting that you happen to be with me tonight?" She made a mock scowl, then smiled. Turning to Nonnie and Jed, she said, "Hi! I'm J.J. Chip and I have been friends for years, but he does have a bit of a wandering eye, you know," she added, winking.

Nonnie laughed. "Boy, isn't that the truth." She glanced up at Jed. "You aren't going to be like that tonight, are you?"

"I'm yours," Jed promised, ignoring the pang of guilt he felt. Another drink would make that go away.

"Hey, look, I'm really glad we spotted you two," Chip said. "This party is getting stale, and we thought we'd go to Max's for a little dancing. Griffith and Cate, and Shelley Goodwin and Tom Arne are going, too. So, what do you say?"

"We'd love to," Nonnie answered, looking prettily at Jed. "Wouldn't we?"

"Sure, why not," Jed said.

"Good." Chip glanced around the crowded room. "We're going to leave as soon as we round up Griffith and Cate. I've got my car, but that'll only fit four." He looked at Jed. "Why don't you two go ahead in a cab, get us a table, and we'll be there in a flash." He snapped his fingers. "Then we'll just all party until they throw us out at closing."

Club Max was packed when they arrived, but Jed wasn't concerned about getting a table. Now that he was considered a regular, tables were easy to get.

They entered the dim, smoke-filled room. Pinpoint spotlights were focused on various couples on the dance floor. As Nonnie led Jed among the closely packed tables, Jed glanced at the dancers. He stopped short. At first he didn't believe what he was seeing. *No, it has to be someone else*, he thought. *Someone who looks like her. After all, what'd Melanie be doing in a place like Club Max?* And, who was that guy she was with? Where could she have met him?

"Jed!" Nonnie cried, coming back for him. "Come on! You can't stand there." Then noticing where Jed was looking, she glanced over as well. "Oh!" she said disgustedly. "Looks like Cole Hillerman has found a new girl to rough up. I swear, I don't understand what girls see in that guy? Know him?"

"No," Jed answered. "Who is he?" He continued to stare at Melanie and Cole. He looked normal enough except for his punk haircut.

"Jed, be serious." Nonnie looked at him. "Surely you've heard of Hillerman Industries." Jed nodded. "Well, Cole is the sort of black sheep son. I think he lives down on Avenue B somewhere. Anyway, he has a reputation for strong arming the girls he dates." She shook her head. "He's slime, okay. Now let's go sit down," she said, tugging at his sleeve.

"No!" Jed said more to himself than to her.
"What do you mean, *no*?"

"That's my sister he's dancing with. I've got to do something about it."

"He's not that bad, Jed," Nonnie corrected. "Leave her alone, she's a big girl. If she's been dating Cole for any length of time, she knows that he likes to play macho."

"Well, he's not going to do it with my sister!" With that, Jed headed toward the dance floor, pushing his way through the jumble of tables that were between him and Melanie.

"Melanie, what's going on here?" Jed demanded as he reached the couple and pulled them apart. Cole let go of Melanie's arm in surprise. "I thought you were supposed to be at a college party?"

"Hey," Cole said, staring coldly at Jed. "Just who do you think you are?" Grabbing Jed, he swung him around so that the two were facing each other. "She's my girl, chump!"

"I'm her brother, creep!" Jed shot back. Yanking himself out from Cole's grasp, he turned back to face Melanie. "Let's go."

"No way!" Melanie said, staring defiantly at Jed. "I'm having a great time!" She wagged her head. "So you can just trot back to whoever—whomever, uh, *whatever*—you're with and leave me alone!" She smiled past Jed at Cole.

"Melanie, have you been drinking?" Jed asked.

"Oh, wow, have I ever," she said, tittering. "And see what fun I'm having."

"That does it!" Jed took Melanie by the arm. "It's pretty obvious that you haven't got the slightest idea what you're doing. How could you end up with a jerk like—"

"*Jerk!*" Cole barked. "I'll show you—"

"Hold it!" A commanding voice and a beefy arm stopped Cole just as he started to take a swing at Jed. "And you, too, sir. I'd like all of you to follow me off the dance floor. Nice and quietly, please." The man was dressed in evening clothes, but beneath the dinner jacket, his muscles bulged. "We don't like scenes here at Club Max." He glanced around at some people who had stopped dancing to gawk. "You people just go on back to having fun. Okay?"

The man kept a firm hold on Cole's arm as they all walked off the dance floor to a quiet corner. There, the man talked with Jed, while a sullen-looking Cole stood silently and a furious Melanie stared at Jed.

A few minutes later, as Melanie went to collect her things, Jed made his way over to Nonnie who was sitting alone at a large table.

"Is everything straightened out?" she asked with bored sarcasm.

"Yes. I'm going to take my sister home."

"Why?" She stared at him. "Why do you have to take her home? She looked okay to me."

Nonnie scowled, but Jed didn't soften a bit. "Look, Jed, your sister's a big girl. She can take care of herself. And she probably won't thank you for dragging her out of here."

"She's my sister, Nonnie, not yours. And I have to do what I think is right. If you want, I can get our cab to drop you off at your place," he offered. "Or back at the party."

"Are you kidding!" Nonnie looked at him. "My night's just beginning. Have you forgotten that our friends are going to be here soon." She tossed her head angrily. "If you feel that you have to play baby-sitter, then go ahead, but I'm staying right here."

Later when the others got there, they asked Nonnie where Jed was. She decided to pay him back for leaving her stranded. "He's gone," she said, flipping her hair off her shoulder in a careless gesture. "I asked him to leave because I couldn't stand the way he was coming on to me. He couldn't keep his hands off me! Can you believe the nerve?" She glanced around at the faces of her friends with immense satisfaction. She could tell that they were eating up every word she told them. She smiled brightly. "Look, as far as I'm concerned, Jed Michaels is history. Anyone want to dance?"

15

Caitlin finally got home at two o'clock on Sunday afternoon. Leaving her luggage by the door in the living room, she tossed her purse and coat on a nearby chair and headed straight for the phone. During the entire flight back from Saint Martin, she had thought about nothing but what she would say to Jed when she called him. She wanted to straighten things out between them right then.

Before she had a chance to dial Jed, her phone rang. She grabbed it up, expecting it to be Jed. "Hello," she said in a cheerful voice.

It was Morgan. "Oh, good, you're back. Caitlin, have you talked to anyone since you got in?"

"No," Caitlin replied, confused. "I just got back a couple minutes ago. Why?"

"Oh, whew!" Morgan said, obviously relieved. "I wanted to make sure I caught you before you spoke to anyone else. Something's happened, Caitlin, and before I tell you, I want you to promise me that you won't believe a word of it. I wouldn't be telling you at all, but I was afraid you would hear it somewhere else and think it was true."

"Morgan, what is it? Please tell me," Caitlin urged. She was beginning to get a very uneasy feeling in her stomach.

"Okay, I'll tell you only if you promise not to go crazy. I know this isn't true, and you will, too, if you really think about it. I mean, we both know that Jed isn't that kind—"

"Morgan!" Caitlin said sharply.

"Okay, okay." Morgan took a deep breath. "Caitlin, there's a rumor going around this morning that Jed spent the night with a blonde named Nonnie Coe last night."

"Wh-what?" Caitlin had been standing, but then she sat down heavily on the couch next to the phone. The uneasy feeling was gone. She felt as if someone had punched her in the stomach. "I knew we were having trouble, but I never thought—"

"See, I knew that's how you'd react. Caitlin, it's a lie, just a vicious lie. Apparently this Nonnie is a real little flirt. I know someone who saw her falling all over Jed at a party earlier," Morgan added. "Caitlin?"

"I'm still here, Morgan. And I guess I believe you. But if there's nothing to the rumor, then how did it get started in the first place?" Caitlin asked.

"Okay, here's the only bad part—Jed did go to Club Max with Nonnie after he left the party. But that's it, that's all there is. It wasn't as if he was alone with her." She paused. "If you don't mind a little advice, I think you should call Jed and talk to him."

"Thanks, Morgan," Caitlin said quietly. "That's exactly what I'm going to do."

For a moment after she hung up, Caitlin let her hand rest on the receiver as she tried to calm down. She was not going to lay into Jed without first giving him a chance to explain. She wasn't! Hadn't she just assured Morgan that she would be rational? Nevertheless, her hand was shaking, as she dialed Jed's number. She let the phone ring twelve times before hanging up. All right, she thought, if Jed was innocent, then why wasn't he home? She began imagining all sorts of horrible scenes—every one of them involving a lovely blonde named Nonnie Coe and Jed.

She called Jed again five minutes later. Still no answer. She called again in another five minutes, with the same result. She was about to try a fourth time when her phone rang. She answered it on the first ring, only to find out it was a wrong number.

Knowing she had to do something to calm herself, she went out into the kitchen and made herself a cup of tea. Carrying it back into the living room, she sat down by the phone again. Taking a sip of her tea, along with several deep breaths, she felt much better. She dialed Jed's number once more.

That time she got through, but it wasn't Jed who answered. Instead, she got a grouchy Melanie.

Remembering her last unhappy confrontation with Jed's sister, she wished she could just hang up. But it was too important that she talk to Jed. "Hello, Melanie, it's Caitlin," she said finally. "Is Jed there?"

"No, he's not," Melanie replied. "Look, Caitlin, I just woke up awhile ago, and I don't feel very well. I've got a horrible headache, and my stomach's upset, and I don't particularly feel like talking to you." She groaned as if to emphasize her words. "So, Caitlin, why don't you just call back?"

"Melanie!" Caitlin barked. "I'm sorry you don't feel well, I really am. But it's very important that I talk to Jed as soon as possible. Do you happen to know where I can reach him?"

"Ummm, not really. He could be anywhere.

All I know is he's not here. As far as I can tell, he hasn't been back since he brought me home last night. Oops, guess I shouldn't have told you that, huh?" she said as she ran her hand sleepily through her hair. "Oh, well, pretend you didn't hear it, okay?" Melanie sounded only vaguely sorry about her slip. "Caitlin, I've really got to go. I think I'm going to be really sick."

"I understand, Melanie. I hope you feel better soon," Caitlin said quietly. "Goodbye."

As she put the phone down, all Caitlin could think of was what a fool she'd been to imagine everything was going to be fine once she was back in New York. How could Jed have done this to her?

The more she thought about it, the more she was convinced that the rumor Morgan had told her really was true. That was why he wasn't at his apartment that morning. Oh, she was furious! Jumping up, she paced to the window and back. She had to do something, but what? She stared hard at the phone and jumped when it suddenly rang.

She reached for it, then hesitated. What if it was Jed? What would she say? She let it ring twice more before finally answering it. It was Jed, and she couldn't think of anything to say. Jed launched into an explanation of what had happened to him the night before.

He told her that he'd gone to a party and that

he'd met some friends there and gone on to Club Max. He told her about finding Melanie and taking her home. "I know you must be thinking some pretty terrible things about me; Melanie said she told you I was out all night. I can imagine what you were thinking. But, honestly, I just slept over at this guy's apartment."

"Oh? So now Nonnie Coe is a *guy*!"

"What? What are you talking about?"

"Nonnie Coe." Caitlin said slowly, exaggerating the syllables. "Everyone's talking about you two," Caitlin said bitterly, "and how you spent the night with her."

"You've got to be joking!" Jed sputtered.

"Would I joke about something like that?" she said flatly.

"But, Caitlin, I was at Bill Strang's house, honest. Call him if you don't believe me. After I took Melanie home, I went out again, but just over to see him. I was upset, and he felt sorry for me and fed me a few drinks. I was so exhausted, I crashed there. Then I came straight back here, and Melanie told me about her conversation with you, so I called you immediately."

"I'm sorry, Jed, I don't believe you," Caitlin said coldy.

"Caitlin, don't do this," Jed persisted. "Can't we at least get together and talk? I can grab a quick shower and be over there in forty-five minutes."

Caitlin sighed. "Don't bother, Jed. It really isn't very important anymore." Her voice sounded suddenly tired. "I'm really exhausted. It was a long weekend, and I worked hard. I've got to go. Goodbye, Jed."

"Cait—"

She replaced the receiver in the cradle and sat looking at it. There was something she couldn't excuse Jed for doing. She couldn't forgive him for changing so much. Jed wasn't the person she had fallen in love with anymore. He was someone else entirely. Somehow, he'd turned into a person she didn't think she could love anymore.

16

In an effort to forget about Jed that next week, Caitlin threw herself into her work. Fortunately Arlene had plenty for her to do. One of her first assignments turned out to be the interview with Brent Lowe that Caitlin thought she had missed. He had been forced to cancel the interview as originally scheduled. When his PR woman had called to change the interview, Caitlin had been available. They had gone to a quiet restaurant on the East Side on Monday night. As they ate, Caitlin asked him dozens of questions, gathering enough material for a fairly in-depth article. She found that she actually liked the handsome young star.

Later, over coffee, he asked Caitlin for a date. "I'll be in New York over Christmas week. Would you go ice-skating with me at Rockefeller

Center?" He had flashed Caitlin the famous smile that would have unglued most young women. "It would give me a really good excuse to hold hands with you," he added shyly.

Laughing lightly, Caitlin shrugged. "I might not be here myself," she said. "I'll probably spend Christmas in Virginia with my grandmother and father. In fact, that's where I'm heading later this week. I'm going home for Thanksgiving weekend."

He looked at her with warm, dark brown eyes. "Too bad. Can I call you when I know my plans just in case yours have changed?"

Caitlin nodded briefly, trying not to think about Jed. "Sure—in case my plans change."

The late-autumn weather was dazzling in Virginia. There was a nip in the air, but it still hadn't gotten terribly cold. Caitlin arrived for Thanksgiving weekend with her jacket slung over her shoulder. It felt wonderful to get away from New York, to pull her thoughts together, and to just relax. It would be just Caitlin, her father, and her grandmother for the main meal on Thursday. But, for once, Caitlin wholeheartedly enjoyed being with her grandmother. It wasn't until they'd nearly finished their dessert course that Caitlin realized why—her grandmother was now treating her like an adult.

Perhaps her new attitude wouldn't last, Caitlin thought, but at least it made the meal more pleasant.

Caitlin's father was busy at his hospital for the rest of the weekend, so Caitlin would be on her own with her grandmother. On Friday she went for a long ride through the back woods of Ryan Acres. The ground was too hard to take any of the jumps safely, so she just hacked. She even let her horse, Duster, take the lead and walk where he pleased for part of the time. It was late when she returned and left Duster with Jeff, the stableman, to be rubbed down and put back in his stall. She spent the rest of the evening working on the first draft of her interview with Brent, hoping that she could have most of it finished by the time she returned to New York on Sunday. Arlene had set the deadline for Tuesday.

She worked on Saturday morning as well. Then because her grandmother had meetings scheduled, she felt a little restless and lonely, so she decided to drive into Georgetown for lunch and some shopping. Changing into navy wool slacks and a pale yellow turtleneck sweater, she pulled on a suede jacket and took off in her new Nissan 280 ZX.

She had just parked outside a restaurant called Samantha's and was walking up the front steps, when she heard footsteps hurrying up behind her. Turning, she nearly bumped into Laurence Baxter. As it turned out, he was on his way in to have a solitary lunch as well.

"Caitlin!" he exclaimed. "I'm so glad I saw you. Will you join me? There's nothing that I'd like better than to have lunch with my favorite ex-girlfriend," he said, referring to the time when they had dated in high school. He smiled. "And, of course, I'm going to pump you about Melanie."

His words made Caitlin's heart sink, but she smiled back. "I'll do my best to fill you in," she said. Suddenly Caitlin wished she could make some excuse to get away, because she knew Laurence would also want to hear about Jed. And Jed was the last person in the world she wanted to talk about.

It turned out to be a difficult lunch. As she ate her sole almondine, Caitlin asked Laurence questions about his work at the newspaper and about his upcoming reassignment from Virginia to Washington, hoping to keep him from mentioning the inevitable. Finally, though, he asked her about Melanie. She was a bit surprised to discover that Laurence had called and talked to Melanie several times. He'd even flown into New York and taken her to the ballet once. "Caitlin, I swear, something could develop between us," Laurence said. "She's a good listener. And she doesn't just say, 'uh-huh' like a lot of

girls when you go on and on about your job."
He paused to smile a moment. "She's really up
on what's happening in the world, too."

"Laurence!" Caitlin cried in surprise. "You
really do like her, don't you?" Caitlin tried to
sound excited, but she also wondered about a
few things. Was Melanie really interested in
Laurence? And if she really did like him, what
about this punk Jed had said he'd seen her with
at that club? Well, she told herself firmly, she
wasn't about to burden Laurence with all of that
unless it became necessary.

"Yes," he said, answering her question, "I
guess I do really like her. In fact, I'd like to spend
Christmas week with her. I haven't told her this
yet, but because of my move to Washington after
the first of the year, the paper's given me two
weeks off. And I'm only going to need one to
pack up my apartment and transfer all my stuff.
I plan to go to New York the other week."

Caitlin nodded, saying she hoped it would all
work out. She loved Laurence like a brother, and
despite Melanie's actions lately, she still was
fond of her.

Caitlin and Laurence said goodbye in the
parking lot. Laurence helped her into her car,
then cheerfully said, "See you in New York"
before carefully shutting her door and waving as
she drove off.

* * *

Caitlin finished the first draft of the interview with Brent Lowe on Sunday morning before she flew back to New York. She typed up the polished version that evening and went to hand it to Arlene the first thing Monday morning. Arlene was in her office chatting with Peter. Caitlin knocked on the partially open door, and Arlene motioned for her to come in.

"This is great, Caitlin," Arlene said after quickly reading through the article. She glanced up from the pages to smile at Caitlin. "If you don't watch out," she said lightly, "you're going to find yourself being asked to write full-time. Then you'll give up working for me."

"Never," Caitlin said, but she was pleased by Arlene's praise.

"No, really," Arlene said, giving a little shake of her head. "I'm serious. You obviously worked very hard on this."

"Then she deserves a night on the town, right?" Peter said. He turned from looking at Arlene, to cocking his head toward Caitlin. "From what I hear, you haven't been anywhere in weeks. Well—" he paused dramatically, a twinkle in his eye—"have I got the party for you! There's a big, opening night bash at Club Central tonight, and my sources tell me that just about everyone's going to be there. Now, you can't say no to that, can you?"

"Well—" Caitlin hesitated. Then she thought it over. It really had been a long time since she had gone out and had a good time. She really was becoming a bit of a drudge. Smiling at Peter, she said, "All right, you talked me into it. I'd love to go."

On her way to the club that night, Caitlin told herself that Peter was right. The party was a big affair. Their cab driver had to wait in line behind several other cabs and limos before finally pulling up in front of the club. As usual a group of curious on-lookers, as well as a few press photographers, had gathered in front of the club. Flashbulbs popped at them as Caitlin and Peter went in. Caitlin was still a bit of a celebrity after her *National* cover, photographs of her being escorted by Peter would no doubt end up in several of the supermarket tabloids the following week.

Caitlin was wearing a silver and white beaded dress that skimmed her figure and ended just above her knees. Over this, she wore a white wool coat lined in silver satin. Her hair was loose and floated about her shoulders in a shiny black cloud. Peter was the perfect escort, handsome in a well-cut dinner jacket.

Inside, a young man took Caitlin's coat for her,

and they were shown into the main room, where the party was already well under way. The music was loud and the dance floor looked packed. Peter order drinks for them both—wine for Caitlin and a gin and tonic for himself. While they were waiting for their drinks to arrive, Peter suggested they dance.

Before long, Caitlin was having a wonderful time. Moving freely to the beat of the music, she felt really relaxed. She smiled and nodded happily when Peter shouted over to her, asking if she was having fun?

But then, as the set ended and they made their way back to their table, Caitlin happened to glance toward the entrance. Her spirits drooped. Jed was standing in the doorway, and he was with Nonnie Coe.

Jed had already seen Caitlin. He had noticed her on the dance floor with Peter moments earlier. And when he had, he was suddenly glad he'd asked Nonnie to come with him.

Sliding his arm around Nonnie's waist, he waited for Caitlin to look their way. Jed felt vaguely uncomfortable using Nonnie the way he was, but she didn't seem to mind. She had obviously forgiven him for leaving her at Club Max, and when he'd asked her to the Club Central opening, she had quickly accepted.

When Caitlin did look his way, he pretended not to see her, smiling down at Nonnie instead.

She really was a knockout, Jed thought distractedly. Sometimes it seemed to him as though no
one was home in her head, but so what, he told
himself—she was gorgeous. On impulse, and
hoping Caitlin was still watching, he bent down
and kissed her neck. That should get to Caitlin,
he thought.

And it did. Caitlin stopped and stood absolutely still at the edge of the dance floor, Peter
behind her. He, too, had seen Jed and Nonnie.
Observing Caitlin wince at the sight of them, he
put his arm around her shoulders and led her to
their table. "Ignore them, Caitlin," he told her in
a low, comforting tone. "They're not worth
getting upset over."

But try as she might, she couldn't forget. She
sat stiffly drinking her wine and trying to listen
as Peter made small talk. Every once in a while,
Caitlin glanced over at Jed and Nonnie, who
were sitting several tables away. Each time she
did, though, it seemed that Jed was getting more
and more cozy with that horrible girl. One time
when she looked over, her gaze met Jed's. She
wasn't certain, but she thought he raised an
eyebrow, mocking her.

It was too much. Caitlin's entire attitude
changed. All right, she thought, two can play at
this game. She would do just as Peter had
suggested, she would ignore Jed. And she
would do it with style. She would not stoop to

using Peter and his feelings for her, but there was no reason why she couldn't be affectionate with him. With a charming smile, she leaned toward Peter and put her hand over his. "Peter," she suggested, "let's dance."

Out on the dance floor, Peter surprised Caitlin by mentioning Nonnie. "Do you know her?" he asked.

"No, just seen her around," Caitlin said. "We don't exactly move in the same circles. I know she gets around a lot, and that she occasionally does some acting on one of the soaps."

"Well, she certainly seems to know you," Peter commented. "She's been glaring at you ever since they arrived." The beat of the music changed, and the band started to play a slow number. Peter pulled Caitlin closer so that she eased into his arms. "She doesn't do it all the time," he said. "Just when she knows Jed isn't paying attention." Peter pulled her even closer to him so that she rested her head on his shoulder. "Be honest with me, Caitlin. Is Jed really your ex-boyfriend, or do you still care for him?"

Caitlin wasn't sure how to answer. Before she could think of anything to say, however, she felt Peter's hand tighten against her back. "What is it?" she asked, suddenly concerned.

"Nonnie and Jed just walked onto the floor,

and it looks as though they're going to be right next to us any second. Better prepare yourself."

"Well, well, well, if it isn't Caitlin Ryan, in person." Nonnie's high-pitched voice rang in Caitlin's ears and she turned her head to see the other girl smiling sweetly at her. Nonnie's eyes, though, were not smiling. "I haven't seen you around lately. But then I don't suppose it's all that easy to find a guy that can replace Jed, is it?"

"Well, I certainly hope Jed doesn't consider *you* a replacement for me!" Caitlin shot back.

"Hah!" Nonnie stared at Caitlin. "You think you're so hot, don't you? Well, you're nothing but a dumb little model. You can't do anything but stand and smile. I, on the other hand, am an actress. My every move makes a statement."

"Oh, really?" Caitlin said, her eyes flashing. "Just remember you said that, I didn't."

"Some actress," Peter added. "I imagine you'll be doing Shakespeare next?"

"Hey!" Jed called out, taking a step toward Peter. "That comment about Nonnie was totally uncalled for."

"Don't get so hot under the collar, Michaels," Peter replied, standing his ground. "I don't want a scene any more than you do. It's that little tramp you brought—"

"*Tramp!*" Nonnie cried, turning a few heads. "You're calling *me* a tramp! Look, I may party a lot, but I don't go off for weekends in the

Caribbean with men." Her eyes narrowed, as she stared viciously at Caitlin. "Now everyone knows exactly how you managed to land the Misty Morn ads, don't they?"

Caitlin flinched. Even though she knew Nonnie's accusations were not true, she could feel people around them judging her. It was finally all too much for her. Angry, embarrassed tears welled up in her eyes. Turning around, she fled from the dance floor.

Seeing Caitlin leave in tears, Peter felt his anger boil over. He turned back to Jed. "Damn you, Michaels. Damn you for hurting her!" Before he could stop himself, he swung with everything he had at Jed.

Jed instinctively blocked the punch. Then, just as instinctively, he got ready to land one on Peter's jaw. But before his fist could make contact, the bouncer stopped it. He had run out onto the floor when he saw the trouble beginning.

And, almost as soon as the near fight had begun, it was over. Peter rushed after Caitlin, and found her putting on her coat. He helped her. Then, slipping his arm comfortingly around her shoulders, they walked toward the club's entrance.

Jed, still on the dance floor, was watching all of this. Seeing Peter put his arms around Caitlin's shoulders made him feel ashamed of himself. He'd only wanted to show Caitlin how it felt to see the person you love with someone else. And he had. But everything had gone wrong so quickly. Damn Nonnie, he thought. She was the one who had started the trouble. If she hadn't shot off her mouth at Caitlin that way, maybe things wouldn't have turned out so terribly.

Just then Nonnie touched his arm. "Want to dance, Jed?" she asked, smiling flirtatiously at him.

He glared down at her. He didn't answer her directly, but instead took her in his arms and they began to move to the music. *All right,* he thought sullenly, *let Caitlin run out on me again. I'll stay. I'll even be the last one to leave. Let Caitlin hear about that!*

17

At her request, Peter took Caitlin straight home from the club. Her tears had stopped by the time they left the club and braved the few reporters still lingering on the sidewalk. A few took pictures of Caitlin and Peter. Holding her head high, Caitlin smiled and looked happy until Peter could get her safely inside a cab. Then she gave a trembling sigh and leaned her head against his shoulder. "Thank you, Peter," she said quietly. And from then until they reached her apartment, she was silent.

Peter left her only after she assured him that she would be all right, that she just wanted to be alone. "I'm fine, honest. I'll probably just go inside and go straight to bed." She kissed Peter's cheek lightly. "I really appreciate all you've done. Thank you, so much."

With Peter gone, Caitlin got ready for bed. Almost in a trance, she slipped out of her dress and hung it on its padded hanger. Then she put on silk pajamas and went into the bathroom where she brushed her teeth, removed her makeup and put moisturizer on her face. Back in the bedroom, she turned down the bed and got in between the fresh sheets, reached over and turned off the light.

But then she lay there for hours, staring at the patterns of light the blinds made on the ceiling. Finally she gave up trying to get to sleep and got up and went into the kitchen. Pouring herself a glass of milk, she took it into the darkened living room. She leaned against the window frame and stared out at the city.

She had to admit after seeing Jed that she still loved him. She was sure they had both been playing games at Club Central earlier. Which meant that Jed still loved her as well. There had to be something she could do to salvage their relationship. But what? If they could only get together and talk—maybe if she called him the first thing in the morning. But, no, that would never work.

Just then the phone rang, making Caitlin jump. The jarring sound only emphasized how alone she was. It had to be Peter, checking up on her to see if she was really all right, she thought, relaxing slightly. But when she crossed the room and turned on the table lamp, she noticed that the clock read five-thirty. Peter would never call at that hour. Picking up the receiver, a shiver of dread ran down her spine. What if Jed had been in an accident? "Hello?"

"Caitlin!" her father said, his voice serious and concerned. "Honey, I'm sorry to be calling you at this hour, but—it's your grandmother. She's ill."

"Grandmother?" Fear clutched at Caitlin.

"Yes," Dr. Westlake went on. "I'm afraid it's quite serious. She's had a stroke."

"Oh, no!" Caitlin gasped. "Is she in the hospital?"

"Yes. In Washington. Honey, I think you should come right away," Dr. Westlake said. "Can you?"

"Yes. Yes, of course." Her mind was swimming. What should she do first? "I'll—I'll take a shuttle flight. But the first one doesn't leave until seven. I'll definitely be on it, though."

"Good girl," her father said, trying to be reassuring. "I'd meet you at Dulles, but I think I'd better stay here with your grandmother." He didn't have to explain. Caitlin knew that he meant that someone should be there in case her grandmother died before she was able to get there. "Take a cab from the airport and when you get to the hospital, come straight to the ICU floor. I'll be waiting for you."

Her father told her the name of the hospital

and hung up. Caitlin sat still, holding the receiver in her hand. She wanted desperately to talk to someone. She wanted to talk to Jed. Pulling the body of the phone closer, she dialed Jed's number.

She let the phone ring for a long, long time before finally admitting that Jed wasn't home.

Then she called Peter. "I'll be right over," he replied when she explained what had happened. "Get dressed, and pack if you need to. Don't worry, I'll get you to the airport."

Peter arrived while Caitlin, already dressed in slacks, a sweater and a wool blazer, was quickly tossing a few things into her overnight bag. When she opened the door and saw him there, she collapsed into his arms and let him comfort her.

Then he took charge, getting her bag and purse from the bedroom, and choosing a camel hair coat from the closet, he helped her into it. He paused then to put his hands on either side of her face and looked into her eyes. "You'll be fine, Caitlin. This is a terrible time for you, but you're strong." He smiled softly. "I know you'll be okay." He kissed her gently on her forehead. "Now come on," he said. "Let's get you to the airport. I have a cab waiting downstairs."

Jed, meanwhile, left Club Central after three to take Nonnie home. When the cab arrived at her apartment, Jed got out, too. He wanted to walk around for a while before going home. When he'd first begun to walk, he wasn't quite sure where he was going. He just aimlessly turned up one street and down the next. But his subconscious must have known where he wanted to be because a few hours later he found himself on Caitlin's street.

During his walk he'd done a lot of thinking. Now, only two blocks from her apartment he was ready to admit to Caitlin—and to anyone else—that he had been wrong. He'd been wrong about school, about his friends, about everything. She was right—he had been wasting his time and his life since he arrived in New York. All he wanted now was to apologize to Caitlin. He loved her, and he just hoped to God that she would forgive him, that she would say she understood, and they they could get back together again.

Quickening his pace, he turned down her block. Looking at his watch, he saw that it was fifteen minutes past six. Caitlin would definitely be asleep, but this was too important. He couldn't wait.

He looked ahead, at the awning in front of her building, and that was when he noticed two people coming out of the entrance. He stopped dead when he realized that one of them was Caitlin. Then he looked at the other person—

Peter Leonard! Sick at heart, Jed dodged into the doorway of a nearby building. There was no way that he wanted either of them to spot him.

He watched as Peter helped Caitlin into a waiting cab, then got in himself. Jed slunk back against the stone wall of the building as the cab pulled away from the curb and sped past him. He continued to stare at the back of the cab until it turned at the corner.

What a fool he'd been! He'd been ready to apologize, after having walked the streets for hours, while Caitlin and Peter—had spent the night together. Well, he'd show her! He'd really show her this time!

18

When Caitlin got off the elevator at the ICU floor, her father was waiting for her. Rushing over to him, she looked anxiously into his face, searching for a sign that he had good news to give her. Gently, he took her hands in his hand and held them tightly.

"She's still in a coma, Caitlin," he explained. "I wish I had better news for you, but I don't. I've talked with the doctor in charge of her case and I'm afraid he's not very hopeful."

"Oh, Father, no." The tears she'd held in check throughout the plane and cab ride began rolling down her cheeks. "There's just so much that's happened lately. I don't want to lose her. I don't."

"I know, honey. I know." Dr. Westlake took Caitlin into his arms and hugged her, letting her sob against his chest. "Look, the doctor said that you can go in and see her, at least briefly. She won't know you're there, but—well, you know—"

"I know." Caitlin raised her head and stared at him with wide, tear-filled eyes. "She might die."

"Yes, I'm afraid so."

Caitlin let out a little hiccuping sob, then wiped the tears from her face. "I do want to go in and see her." She accepted the handkerchief her father had held out to her. "When I come back out, can I talk to her doctor myself?"

"Yes, of course," Dr. Westlake promised. "I know he's in the hospital; I'll ask if he can come up for a few minutes."

Dr. McLanathan, Mrs. Ryan's doctor, turned out to be exceptionally young for someone who had such a wonderful reputation. His face was long and narrow, and he looked as though he rarely smiled. Gravely, he shook Caitlin's hand, then led her to the waiting room where they sat down.

His hazel eyes were just as grave and serious as he spoke to her. "I believe in being perfectly honest with my patient's families. Miss Ryan, your grandmother could die anytime in the next twenty-four hours. On the other hand, there is a chance—a slim one, but still a chance—that her condition could reverse itself. We will just have to wait before I know anything for sure, but the longer she's in the coma, the slimmer her chances of making it are."

"But there *is* a chance?" Caitlin asked, grasping at the few positive words the doctor had told her.

"Yes." He nodded. "But the stroke could also leave her in a permanent coma, or completely paralyzed."

"No, that's impossible," Caitlin said, more to herself than to the doctor. Her grandmother was the most active, alive woman she had ever known. She would never stand for being paralyzed.

"I'm sorry, but it's a very real possibility that you are going to have to face, Miss Ryan." He softened his words slightly. "I'm afraid there really isn't much more you can do right now aside from waiting. If you need me, have them page me. Of course, if there's any major change in your grandmother's condition, I will contact you immediately." He put his hand lightly on hers for a moment, then stood up. He looked down at her. "Is there a number I can call if I need to speak to you?"

"I'll be right here," Caitlin said, nodding numbly. "I'm not leaving."

"I understand." Dr. McLanathan said. Then he gave her a quick smile. "I'll be in touch."

Left alone for a moment, Caitlin looked around her. Sadly she remembered how just a few short months earlier she had spent a long vigil with Jed in a room that was similar to that one. If only Jed were there to be with her. She closed her eyes.

Oh, how she wanted him there. Jed would understand how she felt, what she was going through. She knew that her father cared, and that he would always be there for her, and she appreciated that. But it wasn't the same as having Jed there with her.

She decided to call Jed. After all, hadn't she tried calling him that morning? Now the problems they were having seemed so small, so unimportant. Opening her purse, she searched for a quarter to make the call. She'd noticed that there was a public phone out near the nurse's station and with a tiny feeling of elation she walked over to it. In just a few minutes she would hear his voice.

But although she dialed the long distance number twice, just to be sure she'd reached the right number, there was no answer at Jed's apartment. Feeling even more lost than she had felt a few moments before, she went back to the waiting room.

Dr. Westlake met her in the doorway. "Honey, I'm going to have to run back to Meadow Valley to take care of a few things. Then I'll come back here and be with you, all right?" He looked at her with a weak smile. "I won't be more than a couple of hours, and if you need to call me for any reason, my secretary will reach me wherever I am." He squeezed her shoulder. "I love you, honey. Just keep remembering that."

"I will, Father." Caitlin gave him a shaky smile. "I love you, too. And thanks for staying until I got here."

"I'll always be here for you. I wasn't for the first part of your life, but . . ." He didn't finish because, as they both knew, it was Mrs. Ryan who had kept them apart. "Remember, call if you need me," he said. Then bending down, he kissed her cheek softly before turning to go.

Shortly after Dr. Westlake left, Caitlin called Jed again, but there was no answer. She continued to call his apartment throughout the morning, walking to the phone and placing the call every fifteen or twenty minutes. She would let it ring at least a dozen times, and each time she would wonder again where he could be?

At noon a thoughtful nurse came into the waiting room to suggest to Caitlin that she go to the coffee shop for some lunch. She promised to find Caitlin if there was any change in Mrs. Ryan's condition. Caitlin finally did go and get something to eat, but she barely touched the turkey sandwich she had ordered.

Returning to the ICU floor, she found that her father had called while she was away, leaving a message that he was going to be a bit longer than he'd originally planned. With a sigh, she thanked the nurse who had given her the message and prepared to go back to the waiting room. But then, instead, she decided to try to reach Jed one more time.

Again there was no answer. Feeling totally disheartened she leaned against the wall and put her hand to her forehead, covering her eyes. Why? Why didn't he answer?

19

As Jed watched the cab carrying Caitlin and Peter turn the corner, he suddenly felt exhausted. But he wasn't just physically tired—he was emotionally played out as well. He stumbled back to his apartment, unplugged the phone so he wouldn't be disturbed, and fell into bed without even kicking off his shoes.

When he woke up hours later, it was late afternoon. Feeling slightly disoriented from having slept all day, Jed staggered to his feet and walked slowly into the bathroom, where he stared in complete disgust at his reflection. He hadn't shaved or showered in over twenty-four hours, and his mouth tasted as if someone had walked through it in dirty sneakers.

He let out a strangled, hollow laugh. *Oh, boy, if Caitlin could see me now, she'd never . . .* He didn't finish the thought. He hated Caitlin. He was going to show her that she couldn't make a fool out of him. He stared at himself. She didn't have to make a fool out of him, he decided. He was doing a pretty good job of that all by himself.

Well, to hell with Caitlin, he thought bitterly. To hell with everyone—including Peter Leonard. And Nonnie—he never wanted to see that tramp again. He had to give that one to Peter. He had certainly called it right. She *was* a tramp. She wasn't fit to crawl beneath Caitlin's feet. Damn it! Caitlin again. He had to stop thinking about her. He had to get her completely out of his mind.

With new resolution, he went into the bathroom and turned the shower on full force. He pulled off his clothes and stepped under the needling spray to forget the things he had thought about that morning. That night he needed to get out, to see people, to have fun.

At seven as he was leaving his apartment building, he ran into a group of guys he hadn't seen in a while. They greeted him as if he were a long lost friend and insisted he join them.

"We're on our way to a party," a guy called Biff said. "It's supposed to be kind of an artsy crowd, but is should be fun. It's been going on for twenty-four hours already."

Jed nodded. Sure he'd go. It was just what he

needed—not the girls and the booze. But he did need the noise. He needed lots and lots of noise to help him forget the one person he couldn't seem to stop thinking about. No matter how many places he went, or whom he talked to, he just couldn't get Caitlin out of his mind.

The party was still going strong when Jed and the others arrived. It was at a loft on Tenth Avenue in a neighborhood that was the polar opposite of his own neighborhood. The crowd, too, was a lot rougher than the one that Jed was used to. No one even seemed to know or care who had thrown the party.

One guy explained to Jed that the loft belonged to an artist who was just beginning to make it and was celebrating the opening of his first one-man show. "I don't think he cares what shape he leaves this dump in. He's moving to a better place now that he's got the money." With that, the guy left Jed to talk to some other people.

Left to himself, Jed looked around the room, searching desperately for a familiar face, or at least a friendly one.

Suddenly he saw a familiar face, and he was horrified to realize it was Melanie. What was she doing there? He stared at her. She was drunk again—and with that creep again. Jed knew he'd made it perfectly clear to her that he didn't want her seeing that guy again. He started weaving through the crowd toward her. "Melanie!" he shouted.

She heard him and turned around. *Jed!* "What are you doing here?" she snapped as Jed finally made his way over to her.

"I'm here to save your hide," he hissed. Grabbing her arm, he started escorting her to the door.

"Stop it, Jed," she cried, trying to pull away. "Let me go!"

"You heard her, Jed. Let her go!" Cole demanded in a loud voice. He shoved Jed, forcing him to let go of Melanie's arm.

"And I told *you* that I never wanted you to see my sister again. I meant it, Hillerman!"

"Well, maybe you should see if that's what Melanie wants," Cole replied cockily. "She's old enough to choose who she wants to go out with and who she doesn't. And she happens to have chosen me." Cole's eyes narrowed, he no longer looked cocky, just furious. "So get lost," he threatened. "Leave this party before I have to help you to the door myself."

"Yeah?" Jed scoffed. "You and what army?"

With that, Cole hauled off and swung at Jed. The punch connected, and Jed went flying back against the wall. He managed to right himself just enough to block Cole's next punch, but the next one struck Jed on the side of the head, and that time he went down. The crowd that had gathered around them pulled back, giving the two room. Getting to his knees, Jed launched himself at Cole, managing to tackle him and bring him down. A second later both of them were rolling on the floor, and the fight turned into a wrestling match.

Jed had just managed to pin Cole down when Cole wrestled a hand loose and punched him hard in the ribs. Jed immediately reacted to the pain, letting go of Cole. It took Cole only a moment to act on his advantage. Standing up he pulled Jed to his feet and then, still holding Jed up by the collar, punched his jaw.

Jed tasted blood. He knew that either the next punch, or the one after could knock him unconscious. He thought about Melanie. What would happen to her? Jed tried to fight with renewed energy, but he was too weak to shake off Cole's grip.

But then, suddenly, Cole let him go, and Jed felt someone steadying him. A strong arm continued to support him as he shook his head to clear it. When he turned to see who his angel of mercy was, he was surprised to find it was Peter Leonard. "You!" he cried in a choked voice. "Wh-what are you doing here?"

"At the moment I'm keeping you from getting killed," Peter said. "And now that you're on your feet, let's go get your sister away from that guy."

"Yes," Jed said thickly. "Let's get Melanie." He shook his head once more, feeling better, but not great.

"Good!" Peter nodded. "Let's go."

A few minutes later, with the help of Peter's friend, who happened to be the artist throwing the party, they were all safely out on the street.

Melanie, now that she was out in the cold air, had begun to snap out of her slightly drunken state and was looking sheepish at having caused the terrible fight.

Jed and Peter were still breathing hard and momentarily speechless.

When he caught his breath, Jed still felt awkward. He knew he must thank Peter for helping him and Melanie, but it was hard for him to have to thank the man who'd taken Caitlin away from him. Then as he looked at Peter, the anger he felt toward him began to fade. Just then Peter had proven himself worthy of Caitlin's love. And if Caitlin loved him and was happy with him, then that was what Jed wanted for Caitlin, too. No matter how much it hurt.

Jed was trying to find the right words to express his thoughts to Peter, when Peter spoke up.

"Jed, listen to me"—Peter, still slightly

winded, took in a deep breath, then blew it out again—"something's happened that I think you should know about." Peter then filled Jed in on what had happened with Caitlin's grandmother. "She tried to call you first, but you weren't home," Peter explained. "So she called me. And I went over and took her to the airport."

So that was what Peter was doing at Caitlin's apartment this morning, Jed thought, suddenly realizing how stupid he'd been to jump to the conclusion that Peter had spent the night with her. But then Jed became furious with himself that he hadn't known, that he hadn't been there for Caitlin. "Why didn't you say something to me about this earlier?"

"Come on, Jed, I didn't even know you were here!"

"No," Jed admitted. "Of course you didn't."

"Well, now you know." Peter put a hand on Jed's shoulder. "And, if I were the one Caitlin loved, I wouldn't waste any more time standing here. I'd get to the airport as fast as I could. You can just make the last shuttle to Washington."

"That's exactly what I'm going to do," Jed said. But then he remembered Melanie; he couldn't leave her there.

Peter read Jed's expression. "Don't worry. I'll see to it that your sister gets home all right." He glanced down the street. "Look, there's a cab now. You take it, we'll get the next one."

"Thanks!" Jed said sincerely, putting his hand on Peter's shoulder. "Thanks for everything."

"My pleasure," Peter replied. Then he smiled wryly and added, "I think."

Jed sat in the back of the cab while it sped through streets and across the East River toward the airport. His mind was totally engulfed by thoughts of Caitlin. No matter what should happen between them, he just knew that he had to get there in time, to be with her when she needed him.

20

Caitlin was alone in the waiting room, crying softly. Until a few moments earlier her father had been there with her. Then Dr. McLanathan had come to the door and motioned for Dr. Westlake to join him. They had spoken in low voices, so that she couldn't hear their short conversation. Her father had nodded, the expression on his face grave. Then they both left the room, stopping to tell Caitlin they would be back soon.

She was absolutely convinced that her grandmother was dying. Mrs. Ryan was still in the coma, and if she didn't come out of it soon, her chances of survival would decrease. Wiping her cheeks, Caitlin told herself that she must not break down. But all she wanted to do was sob out loud. And she wanted someone's shoulder to lean on. She wanted that someone to be Jed.

She wanted his arms around her, comforting her. Oh, why wasn't he there? Fresh tears began to slide down her cheeks.

In her desolation, she didn't hear the quiet footsteps coming up to her, didn't know anyone was beside her until she felt a hand on her shoulder. Then she looked up.

"Jed?" she cried, not quite trusting her eyes at first. "Jed! Oh, Jed!" She threw herself into his arms.

"I came as soon as I heard," he said, softly, his mouth against her ear. "Peter told me."

"Jed, Oh, Jed," she sobbed. "I kept wishing you were here—and—" she said, sniffling.

"I'm here," he said gently. "And I'm not going to leave you again." He continued to hold her for a long, silent moment, his hand moving slowly over her back, comforting her.

At last she sighed and pulled back to look up at him. "Jed, I'm so very sorry about the way I've been these last months. I don't think I really realized just what you were going through with the loss of your father, until I heard about my grandmother. I should have been so much more understanding." She looked at him hopefully. "Will you ever forgive me?"

"Caitlin, I'm the one who should be asking your forgiveness." He shook his head. "You were right all along. I should have straightened myself out. I know now just how, well, childish

I've been. I wasted so much time." A pained look came into his eyes. "And I almost lost you. Oh, God, Caitlin," his voice trembled. "How could I ever let that almost happen?" He pulled her tight against him, cupping her head to his chest, as he kissed her hair. "I love you so, so very much, my darling."

"And I love you, Jed," she cried softly, closing her eyes and resting her cheek against the slight roughness of his wool jacket.

It was then that Dr. Westlake came into the room. He stood in the doorway for a moment, then cleared his throat. "Caitlin?" he called in a low voice.

"Yes?" She broke away from Jed to look at her father, her eyes mirroring the fearful question she was unable to put into words.

"She's going to be fine," Dr. Westlake announced. "She's out of the coma." He smiled. "I've told her you're here, and she wants to see you. You can go in and see her whenever you're ready."

"Oh, Father, that's wonderful!" Caitlin's face lit up. She turned to Jed. "Isn't that wonderful?" she asked happily.

"Yes, truly wonderful," Jed agreed.

"Oh, my God, Jed!" she cried, looking at him, her eyes clouded with sudden concern. "How did you hurt yourself?" She shook her head. "I must have been so excited about seeing you that

I didn't notice those bruises on your face until now." She put her hand up and gently touched the side of his jaw with her fingers. "Does it hurt?"

"Actually it does hurt." He'd been so concerned about Caitlin that he'd almost forgotten that Cole had hit him. "No, it's not really all that bad," he said ruefully. "I guess I could say that this was part of learning my lesson—the hard way."

"I don't understand." She looked at him questioningly.

"Don't worry. I'll tell you about it later." He grinned again, this time in absolute happiness. "After you've seen your grandmother."

"Is that a promise?" she asked.

"It's a firm promise," he told her in a low voice that was filled with love. Then, as Dr. Westlake tactfully turned his back to them, Jed took her in his arms once again and sealed his promise with a kiss.

FRANCINE PASCAL

In addition to collaborating on the Broadway musical *George M!* and the nonfiction book *The Strange Case of Patty Hearst*, Francine Pascal has written an adult novel, *Save Johanna!*, and four young adult novels, *Hangin' Out with Cici*, *My First Love and Other Disasters*, *The Hand-Me-Down Kid*, and *Love and Betrayal & Hold the Mayo!* She is also the creator of the Sweet Valley High and Sweet Valley Twins series. Ms. Pascal has three daughters, Jamie, Susan, and Laurie, and lives in New York City.

DIANA GREGORY

Growing up in Hollywood, Diana Gregory wanted to become an actress. She became an associate TV producer instead. Now a full-time writer, she has written, in addition to other books, three young adult novels, *I'm Boo! That's Who!*, *There's a Caterpillar in My Lemonade*, and *The Fog Burns Off by Eleven O'clock*, plus several Sweet Dreams novels. Besides writing, her other love is traveling. She has lived in several states, including Virginia, where she stayed on a horse farm for a year. She now calls Seattle home.

CAITLIN'S BACK!

Caitlin, the unforgettable and beautiful star of
Loving, Love Lost, and *True Love,* is back in

THE PROMISE TRILOGY

Three new books that promise all the romance and excitement
you could ever ask for.

☐   25812/$2.95
TENDER PROMISES—Caitlin and her boyfriend Jed are off
to spend the summer in Montana. But there's trouble ahead when
Jed's ex-girlfriend makes a play to get him back. Can Caitlin
and Jed's tender promises of love survive this test?

☐   26156/$2.95
PROMISES BROKEN—At college, Julian's plot to break up
Jed and Caitlin succeeds and Julian grabs the chance to try
to make Caitlin fall in love with him. Can he find his way into
Caitlin's broken heart?

☐   26194/$2.95
A NEW PROMISE—Caitlin is Julian's girl now ... Jed is just
a name in her past—until Julian's nasty schemes are finally
revealed. Now that Jed and Caitlin know the truth, can they find
a new promise of love together?

**Caitlin—you loved her first three books, from
THE LOVE TRILOGY—don't miss out on
THE PROMISE TRILOGY.**

Prices and availability subject to change without notice.

Buy them at your local bookstore or use this handy coupon for ordering:

Bantam Books, Dept. CI5, 414 East Golf Road, Des Plaines, Ill. 60016

Please send me the books I have checked above. I am enclosing $_____ (please
add $1.50 to cover postage and handling). Send check or money order—no cash
or C.O.D.s please.

Mr/Ms _____

Address _____

City/State _____ Zip _____

                                                                CI5—2/88

Please allow four to six weeks for delivery. This offer expires 8/88.

Get Ready for a Thrilling Time in Sweet Valley®!

☐ **26905 DOUBLE JEOPARDY #1** $2.95

When the twins get part-time jobs on the Sweet Valley newspaper, they're in for some chilling turn of events. The "scoops" Jessica invents to impress a college reporter turn into the real thing when she witnesses an actual crime—but now no one will believe her! The criminal has seen her car, and now he's going after Elizabeth ... the twins have faced danger and adventure before ... but never like this!

Prices and availability subject to change without notice.

Buy them at your local bookstore or use this handy coupon for ordering:

Bantam Books, Inc., Dept. SVH4, 414 East Golf Road, Des Plaines, IL 60016

Please send me the books i have checked above. I am enclosing $_____ (please add $1.50 to cover postage and handling). Send check or money order—no cash or C.O.D.s please.

Mr/Ms _____

Address _____

City/State _____ Zip _____

SVH4—12/87

Please allow four to six weeks for delivery. This offer expires 6/88.

SWEET VALLEY HIGH

*Celebrate the Seasons
with SWEET VALLEY HIGH
Super Editions*

You've been a SWEET VALLEY HIGH fan all along—hanging out with Jessica and Elizabeth and their friends at Sweet Valley High. And now the SWEET VALLEY HIGH *Super Editions* give you more of what you like best—more romance—more excitement—more real-life adventure! Whether you're bicycling up the California Coast in PERFECT SUMMER, dancing at the Sweet Valley Christmas Ball in SPECIAL CHRISTMAS, touring the South of France in SPRING BREAK, catching the rays in a MALIBU SUMMER, or skiing the snowy slopes in WINTER CARNIVAL—you know you're exactly where you want to be—with the gang from SWEET VALLEY HIGH.

SWEET VALLEY HIGH SUPER EDITIONS

☐ PERFECT SUMMER
25072/$2.95

☐ SPRING BREAK
25537/$2.95

☐ SPECIAL CHRISTMAS
25377/$2.95

☐ MALIBU SUMMER
26050/$2.95

☐ WINTER CARNIVAL
26159/$2.95

☐ SPRING FEVER
26420/$2.95

Prices and availability subject to change without notice.

Bantam Books, Dept. SVS2, 414 East Golf Road, Des Plaines, IL 60016

Please send me the books I have checked above. I am enclosing $_____ (please add $1.50 to cover postage and handling). Send check or money order—no cash or C.O.D.s please.

Mr/Ms _____

Address _____

City/State _____ Zip _____

SVS2—2/88

Please allow four to six weeks for delivery. This offer expires 8/88.

BANTAM
SHOP-AT-HOME
C·A·T·A·L·O·G

Special Offer
Buy a Bantam Book
for only 50¢.

Now you can have Bantam's catalog filled with hundreds of titles plus take advantage of our unique and exciting bonus book offer. A special offer which gives you the opportunity to purchase a Bantam book for only 50¢. Here's how!

By ordering any five books at the regular price per order, you can also choose any other single book listed (up to a $5.95 value) for just 50¢. Some restrictions do apply, but for further details why not send for Bantam's catalog of titles today!

Just send us your name and address and we will send you a catalog!

BANTAM BOOKS, INC.
P.O. Box 1006, South Holland, Ill. 60473

Mr./Mrs./Ms. _____
(please print)

Address _____

City _____ State _____ Zip _____
FC(A)—10/87
Please allow four to six weeks for delivery.